LASTI

Maupassant Original Short Stories

Volume X

Guy de Maupassant

iBoo Press
London

LASTING LOVE

Maupasant Original Short Stories

Volume X

Guy de Maupassant

Translated by
ALBERT M. C. McMASTER, B.A.
A. E. HENDERSON, B.A.
MME. QUESADA and Others

Layout & Cover © Copyright 2020 iBooPress, London

Published by
iBoo Press House

3rd Floor
86-90 Paul Street
London, EC2A4NE UK

t: +44 20 3695 0809
info@iboo.com II iBoo.com

ISBN
978-1-64181-748-6 (p)

LASTING LOVE

Maupasant Original Short Stories

Volume X

Guy de Maupassant

VOLUME X

THE CHRISTENING 7

THE FARMER'S WIFE 11

THE DEVIL 17

THE SNIPE 23

THE WILL 25

WALTER SCHNAFFS' ADVENTURE 30

AT SEA 37

MINUET 42

THE SON 46

THAT PIG OF A MORIN 54

SAINT ANTHONY 63

LASTING LOVE 70

PIERROT 75

A NORMANDY JOKE 80

FATHER MATTHEW 84

VOLUME X

THE CHRISTENING
THE MARVELLOUS NOTE
CHEDDER
THE SALT
THE WELL
WALTER SCHNAFFS' ADVENTURE
AT SEA
MINUET
THE SON
THAT YEAR A WARM
SAINT ANTHONY
LASTING LOVE
PIERROT
A NORMANDY JOKE
FATHER MATTHEW

THE CHRISTENING

"Well doctor, a little brandy?"

"With pleasure."

The old ship's surgeon, holding out his glass, watched it as it slowly filled with the golden liquid. Then, holding it in front of his eyes, he let the light from the lamp stream through it, smelled it, tasted a few drops and smacked his lips with relish. Then he said:

"Ah! the charming poison! Or rather the seductive murderer, the delightful destroyer of peoples!

"You people do not know it the way I do. You may have read that admirable book entitled L'Assommoir, but you have not, as I have, seen alcohol exterminate a whole tribe of savages, a little kingdom of negroes—alcohol calmly unloaded by the barrel by red-bearded English seamen.

"Right near here, in a little village in Brittany near Pont-l'Abbe, I once witnessed a strange and terrible tragedy caused by alcohol. I was spending my vacation in a little country house left me by my father. You know this flat coast where the wind whistles day and night, where one sees, standing or prone, these giant rocks which in the olden times were regarded as guardians, and which still retain something majestic and imposing about them. I always expect to see them come to life and start to walk across the country with the slow and ponderous tread of giants, or to unfold enormous granite wings and fly toward the paradise of the Druids.

"Everywhere is the sea, always ready on the slightest provocation to rise in its anger and shake its foamy mane at those bold enough to brave its wrath.

"And the men who travel on this terrible sea, which, with one motion of its green back, can overturn and swallow up their frail barks—they go out in the little boats, day and night, hardy, weary and drunk. They are often drunk. They have a saying which says: 'When the bottle is full you see the reef, but when it is empty you see it no more.'

"Go into one of their huts; you will never find the father there. If you ask the woman what has become of her husband, she will stretch her arms out over the dark ocean which rumbles and roars along the coast. He remained, there one night, when he had had too much to drink; so did her oldest son. She has four more big, strong, fair-haired boys. Soon it will be their time.

"As I said, I was living in a little house near Pont-l'Abbe. I was there alone with my servant, an old sailor, and with a native family which took care of the grounds in my absence. It consisted of three persons, two sisters and a man, who had married one of them, and who attended to the garden.

"A short time before Christmas my gardener's wife presented him with a boy. The husband asked me to stand as god-father. I could hardly deny the request, and so he borrowed ten francs from me for the cost of the christening, as he said.

"The second day of January was chosen as the date of the ceremony. For a week the earth had been covered by an enormous white carpet of snow, which made this flat, low country seem vast and limitless. The ocean appeared to be black in contrast with this white plain; one could see it rolling, raging and tossing its waves as though wishing to annihilate its pale neighbor, which appeared to be dead, it was so calm, quiet and cold.

"At nine o'clock the father, Kerandec, came to my door with his sister-in-law, the big Kermagan, and the nurse, who carried the infant wrapped up in a blanket. We started for the church. The weather was so cold that it seemed to dry up the skin and crack it open. I was thinking of the poor little creature who was being carried on ahead of us, and I said to myself that this Breton race must surely be of iron, if their children were able, as soon as they were born, to stand such an outing.

"We came to the church, but the door was closed; the priest was late.

"Then the nurse sat down on one of the steps and began to undress the child. At first I thought there must have been some slight accident, but I saw that they were leaving the poor little fellow naked completely naked, in the icy air. Furious at such imprudence, I protested:

"'Why, you are crazy! You will kill the child!'

"The woman answered quietly: 'Oh, no, sir; he must wait naked before the Lord.'

"The father and the aunt looked on undisturbed. It was the custom. If it were not adhered to misfortune was sure to attend the little one.

"I scolded, threatened and pleaded. I used force to try to cover the frail creature. All was in vain. The nurse ran away from me through the snow, and the body of the little one turned purple. I was about to leave these brutes when I saw the priest coming across the country, followed. by the sexton and a young boy. I ran towards him and gave vent to my indignation. He showed no surprise nor did he quicken his pace in the least. He answered:

"'What can you expect, sir? It's the custom. They all do it, and it's of no use trying to stop them.'

"'But at least hurry up!' I cried.

"He answered: 'But I can't go any faster.'

"He entered the vestry, while we remained outside on the church steps. I was suffering. But what about the poor little creature who was howling from the effects of the biting cold.

"At last the door opened. He went into the church. But the poor child had to remain naked throughout the ceremony. It was interminable. The priest stammered over the Latin words and mispronounced them horribly. He walked slowly and with a ponderous tread. His white surplice chilled my heart. It seemed as though, in the name of a pitiless and barbarous god, he had wrapped himself in another kind of snow in order to torture this little piece of humanity that suffered so from the cold.

"Finally the christening was finished according to the rites and I saw the nurse once more take the frozen, moaning child and wrap it up in the blanket.

"The priest said to me: 'Do you wish to sign the register?'

"Turning to my gardener, I said: 'Hurry up and get home quickly so that you can warm that child.' I gave him some advice so as to ward off, if not too late, a bad attack of pneumonia. He promised to follow my instructions and left with his sister-in-law and the nurse. I followed the priest into the vestry, and when I had signed he demanded five francs for expenses.

"As I had already given the father ten francs, I refused to pay twice. The priest threatened to destroy the paper and to annul the ceremony. I, in turn, threatened him with the district attorney. The dispute was long, and I finally paid five francs.

"As soon as I reached home I went down to Kerandec's to find out whether everything was all right. Neither father, nor sister-in-law, nor nurse had yet returned. The mother, who had remained alone, was in bed, shivering with cold and starving, for she had had nothing to eat since the day before.

"'Where the deuce can they have gone?' I asked. She answered without surprise or anger, 'They're going to drink something to celebrate: It was the custom. Then I thought, of my ten francs which were to pay the church and would doubtless pay for the alcohol.

"I sent some broth to the mother and ordered a good fire to be built in the room. I was uneasy and furious and promised myself to drive out these brutes, wondering with terror what was going to happen to the poor infant.

"It was already six, and they had not yet returned. I told my servant to wait for them and I went to bed. I soon fell asleep and slept like a top. At daybreak I was awakened by my servant, who was bringing me my hot water.

"As soon as my eyes were open I asked: 'How about Kerandec?'

"The man hesitated and then stammered: 'Oh! he came back, all right, after midnight, and so drunk that he couldn't walk, and so were Kermagan and the nurse. I guess they must have slept in a ditch, for the little one died and they never even noticed it.'

"I jumped up out of bed, crying:

"'What! The child is dead?'

"'Yes, sir. They brought it back to Mother Kerandec. When she saw it she began to cry, and now they are making her drink to console her.'

"'What's that? They are making her drink!'

"'Yes, sir. I only found it out this morning. As Kerandec had no more brandy or money, he took some wood alcohol, which monsieur gave him for the lamp, and all four of them are now drinking that. The mother is feeling pretty sick now.'

"I had hastily put on some clothes, and seizing a stick, with the intention of applying it to the backs of these human beasts, I hastened towards the gardener's house.

"The mother was raving drunk beside the blue body of her dead baby. Kerandec, the nurse, and the Kermagan woman were snoring on the floor. I had to take care of the mother, who died towards noon."

The old doctor was silent. He took up the brandy-bottle and poured out another glass. He held it up to the lamp, and the light streaming through it imparted to the liquid the amber color of molten topaz. With one gulp he swallowed the treacherous drink.

THE FARMER'S WIFE

Said the Baron Rene du Treilles to me:

"Will you come and open the hunting season with me at my farm at Marinville? I shall be delighted if you will, my dear boy. In the first place, I am all alone. It is rather a difficult ground to get at, and the place I live in is so primitive that I can invite only my most intimate friends."

I accepted his invitation, and on Saturday we set off on the train going to Normandy. We alighted at a station called Almivare, and Baron Rene, pointing to a carryall drawn by a timid horse and driven by a big countryman with white hair, said:

"Here is our equipage, my dear boy."

The driver extended his hand to his landlord, and the baron pressed it warmly, asking:

"Well, Maitre Lebrument, how are you?"

"Always the same, M'sieu le Baron."

We jumped into this swinging hencoop perched on two enormous wheels, and the young horse, after a violent swerve, started into a gallop, pitching us into the air like balls. Every fall backward on the wooden bench gave me the most dreadful pain.

The peasant kept repeating in his calm, monotonous voice:

"There, there! All right all right, Moutard, all right!"

But Moutard scarcely heard, and kept capering along like a goat.

Our two dogs behind us, in the empty part of the hencoop, were standing up and sniffing the air of the plains, where they scented game.

The baron gazed with a sad eye into the distance at the vast Norman landscape, undulating and melancholy, like an immense English park, where the farmyards, surrounded by two or four rows of trees and full of dwarfed apple trees which hid the houses, gave a vista as far as the eye could see of forest trees, copses and shrubbery such as landscape gardeners look for in laying out the boundaries of princely estates.

And Rene du Treilles suddenly exclaimed:

"I love this soil; I have my very roots in it."

He was a pure Norman, tall and strong, with a slight paunch, and of the old race of adventurers who went to found kingdoms on the shores of every ocean. He was about fifty years of age, ten years less perhaps than the farmer who was driving us.

The latter was a lean peasant, all skin and bone, one of those men who live a hundred years.

After two hours' travelling over stony roads, across that green and monotonous plain, the vehicle entered one of those orchard farmyards and drew up before in old structure falling into decay, where an old maid-servant stood waiting beside a young fellow, who took charge of the horse.

We entered the farmhouse. The smoky kitchen was high and spacious. The copper utensils and the crockery shone in the reflection of the hearth. A cat lay asleep on a chair, a dog under the table. One perceived an odor of milk, apples, smoke, that indescribable smell peculiar to old farmhouses; the odor of the earth, of the walls, of furniture, the odor of spilled stale soup, of former wash-days and of former inhabitants, the smell of animals and of human beings combined, of things and of persons, the odor of time, and of things that have passed away.

I went out to have a look at the farmyard. It was very large, full of apple trees, dwarfed and crooked, and laden with fruit which fell on the grass around them. In this farmyard the Norman smell of apples was as strong as that of the bloom of orange trees on the shores of the south of France.

Four rows of beeches surrounded this inclosure. They were so tall that they seemed to touch the clouds at this hour of nightfall, and their summits, through which the night winds passed, swayed and sang a mournful, interminable song.

I reentered the house.

The baron was warming his feet at the fire, and was listening to the farmer's talk about country matters. He talked about marriages, births and deaths, then about the fall in the price of grain and the latest news about cattle. The "Veularde" (as he called a cow that had been bought at the fair of Veules) had calved in the middle of June. The cider had not been first-class last year. Apricots were almost disappearing from the country.

Then we had dinner. It was a good rustic meal, simple and abundant, long and tranquil. And while we were dining I noticed the special kind of friendly familiarity which had struck me from the start between the baron and the peasant.

Outside, the beeches continued sighing in the night wind, and our two dogs, shut up in a shed, were whining and howling in an uncanny fashion. The fire was dying out in the big fireplace. The maid-servant had gone to bed. Maitre Lebrument said in his turn:

"If you don't mind, M'sieu le Baron, I'm going to bed. I am not used to staying up late."

The baron extended his hand toward him and said: "Go, my friend," in so cordial a tone that I said, as soon as the man had disappeared:

"He is devoted to you, this farmer?"

"Better than that, my dear fellow! It is a drama, an old drama, simple and very sad, that attaches him to me. Here is the story:

"You know that my father was colonel in a cavalry regiment. His orderly was this young fellow, now an old man, the son of a farmer. When my father retired from the army he took this former soldier, then about forty; as his servant. I was at that time about thirty. We were living in our old chateau of Valrenne, near Caudebec-en-Caux.

"At this period my mother's chambermaid was one of the prettiest girls you could see, fair-haired, slender and sprightly in manner, a genuine soubrette of the old type that no longer exists. Today these creatures spring up into hussies before their time. Paris, with the aid of the railways, attracts them, calls them, takes hold of them, as soon as they are budding into womanhood, these little sluts who in old times remained simple maid-servants. Every man passing by, as recruiting sergeants did formerly, looking for recruits, with conscripts, entices and ruins them —these foolish lassies—and we have now only the scum of the female sex for servant maids, all that is dull, nasty, common and ill-formed, too ugly, even for gallantry.

"Well, this girl was charming, and I often gave her a kiss in dark corners; nothing more, I swear to you! She was virtuous, besides; and I had some respect for my mother's house, which is more than can be said of the blackguards of the present day.

"Now, it happened that my man-servant, the ex-soldier, the old farmer you have just seen, fell madly in love with this girl, perfectly daft. The first thing we noticed was that he forgot everything, he paid no attention to anything.

"My father said incessantly:

"'See here, Jean, what's the matter with you? Are you ill?'

"He replied:

"'No, no, M'sieu le Baron. There's nothing the matter with me.'

"He grew thin; he broke glasses and let plates fall when waiting on the table. We thought he must have been attacked by some nervous affection, and sent for the doctor, who thought he could detect symptoms of spinal disease. Then my father, full of anxiety about his faithful man-servant, decided to place him in a private hospital. When the poor fellow heard of my father's intentions he made a clean breast of it.

"'M'sieu le Baron'

"'Well, my boy?'

"'You see, the thing I want is not physic.'

"'Ha! what is it, then?'

"'It's marriage!'

"My father turned round and stared at him in astonishment.

"'What's that you say, eh?'

"'It's marriage.'"

"'Marriage! So, then, you jackass, you're to love.'

"'That's how it is, M'sieu le Baron.'

"And my father began to laugh so immoderately that my mother called out through the wall of the next room:

"'What in the world is the matter with you, Gontran?'

"He replied:

"'Come here, Catherine.'

"And when she came in he told her, with tears in his eyes from sheer laughter, that his idiot of a servant-man was lovesick.

"But my mother, instead of laughing, was deeply affected.

"'Who is it that you have fallen in love with, my poor fellow?' she asked.

"He answered without hesitation:

"'With Louise, Madame le Baronne.'

"My mother said with the utmost gravity: 'We must try to arrange this matter the best way we can.'

"So Louise was sent for and questioned by my mother; and she said in reply that she knew all about Jean's liking for her, that in fact Jean had spoken to her about it several times, but that she did not want him. She refused to say why.

"And two months elapsed during which my father and mother never ceased to urge this girl to marry Jean. As she declared she was not in love with any other man, she could not give any serious reason for her refusal. My father at last overcame her resistance by means of a big present of money, and started the pair of them on a farm—this very farm. I did not see them for three years, and then I learned that Louise had died of consumption. But my father and mother died, too, in their turn, and it was two years more before I found myself face to face with Jean.

"At last one autumn day about the end of October the idea came into my head to go hunting on this part of my estate, which my father had told me was full of game.

14

"So one evening, one wet evening, I arrived at this house. I was shocked to find my father's old servant with perfectly white hair, though he was not more than forty-five or forty-six years of age. I made him dine with me, at the very table where we are now sitting. It was raining hard. We could hear the rain battering at the roof, the walls, and the windows, flowing in a perfect deluge into the farmyard; and my dog was howling in the shed where the other dogs are howling to-night.

"All of a sudden, when the servant-maid had gone to bed, the man said in a timid voice:

"'M'sieu le Baron.'

"'What is it, my dear Jean?'

"'I have something to tell you.'

"'Tell it, my dear Jean.'

"'You remember Louise, my wife.'

"'Certainly, I remember her.'

"'Well, she left me a message for you.'

"'What was it?'

"'A—a—well, it was what you might call a confession.'

"'Ha—and what was it about?'

"'It was—it was—I'd rather, all the same, tell you nothing about it—but I must—I must. Well, it's this—it wasn't consumption she died of at all. It was grief—well, that's the long and short of it. As soon as she came to live here after we were married, she grew thin; she changed so that you wouldn't know her, M'sieu le Baron. She was just as I was before I married her, but it was just the opposite, just the opposite.

"'I sent for the doctor. He said it was her liver that was affected—he said it was what he called a "hepatic" complaint—I don't know these big words, M'sieu le Baron. Then I bought medicine for her, heaps on heaps of bottles that cost about three hundred francs. But she'd take none of them; she wouldn't have them; she said: "It's no use, my poor Jean; it wouldn't do me any good." I saw well that she had some hidden trouble; and then I found her one time crying, and I didn't know what to do, no, I didn't know what to do. I bought her caps, and dresses, and hair oil, and earrings. Nothing did her any good. And I saw that she was going to die. And so one night at the end of November, one snowy night, after she had been in bed the whole day, she told me to send for the cure. So I went for him. As soon as he came—'

"'Jean,' she said, 'I am going to make a confession to you. I owe it to you, Jean. I have never been false to you, never! never, before or after you married me. M'sieu le Cure is there, and can tell you so; he knows my soul. Well, listen, Jean. If I am dying, it is because I was not able to console myself for leaving the chateau, because I was too fond of the young Baron Monsieur Rene, too fond of him, mind you, Jean, there was no harm in it! This is the thing that's killing me. When I could see him no more I felt that I should die. If I could only have seen him, I might have lived, only seen him, nothing more. I wish you'd tell him some day, by and by, when I am no longer here. You will tell him, swear you, will, Jean—swear it—in the presence of M'sieu le Cure! It will console me to know that he will know it one day, that this was the cause of my death! Swear it!'

"'Well, I gave her my promise, M'sieu le Baron, and on the faith of an honest man I have kept my word.'

"And then he ceased speaking, his eyes filling with tears.

"Good God! my dear boy, you can't form any idea of the emotion that filled me when I heard this poor devil, whose wife I had killed without suspecting it, telling me this story on that wet night in this very kitchen.

"I exclaimed: 'Ah! my poor Jean! my poor Jean!'

"He murmured: 'Well, that's all, M'sieu le Baron. I could not help it, one way or the other—and now it's all over!'

"I caught his hand across the table, and I began to weep.

"He asked, 'Will you come and see her grave?' I nodded assent, for I couldn't speak. He rose, lighted a lantern, and we walked through the blinding rain by the light of the lantern.

"He opened a gate, and I saw some crosses of black wood.

"Suddenly he stopped before a marble slab and said: 'There it is,' and he flashed the lantern close to it so that I could read the inscription:

"'TO LOUISE HORTENSE MARINET,

"'Wife of Jean-Francois Lebrument, Farmer,

"'SHE WAS A FAITHFUL WIFE. GOD REST HER SOUL.'

"We fell on our knees in the damp grass, he and I, with the lantern between us, and I saw the rain beating on the white marble slab. And I thought of the heart of her sleeping there in her grave. Ah! poor heart! poor heart! Since then I come here every year. And I don't know why, but I feel as if I were guilty of some crime in the presence of this man who always looks as if he forgave me."

THE DEVIL

The peasant and the doctor stood on opposite sides of the bed, beside the old, dying woman. She was calm and resigned and her mind quite clear as she looked at them and listened to their conversation. She was going to die, and she did not rebel at it, for her time was come, as she was ninety-two.

The July sun streamed in at the window and the open door and cast its hot flames on the uneven brown clay floor, which had been stamped down by four generations of clodhoppers. The smell of the fields came in also, driven by the sharp wind and parched by the noontide heat. The grass-hoppers chirped themselves hoarse, and filled the country with their shrill noise, which was like that of the wooden toys which are sold to children at fair time.

The doctor raised his voice and said: "Honore, you cannot leave your mother in this state; she may die at any moment." And the peasant, in great distress, replied: "But I must get in my wheat, for it has been lying on the ground a long time, and the weather is just right for it; what do you say about it, mother?" And the dying old woman, still tormented by her Norman avariciousness, replied yes with her eyes and her forehead, and thus urged her son to get in his wheat, and to leave her to die alone.

But the doctor got angry, and, stamping his foot, he said: "You are no better than a brute, do you hear, and I will not allow you to do it, do you understand? And if you must get in your wheat today, go and fetch Rapet's wife and make her look after your mother; I will have it, do you understand me? And if you do not obey me, I will let you die like a dog, when you are ill in your turn; do you hear?"

The peasant, a tall, thin fellow with slow movements, who was tormented by indecision, by his fear of the doctor and his fierce love of saving, hesitated, calculated, and stammered out: "How much does La Rapet charge for attending sick people?" "How should I know?" the doctor cried. "That depends upon how long she is needed. Settle it with her, by Heaven! But I want her to be here within an hour, do you hear?"

So the man decided. "I will go for her," he replied; "don't get angry, doctor." And the latter left, calling out as he went: "Be careful, be very careful, you know, for I do not joke when I am angry!" As soon as they were alone the peasant turned to his mother and said in a resigned voice: "I will go and fetch La Rapet, as the man will have it. Don't worry till I get back."

And he went out in his turn.

La Rapet, old was an old washerwoman, watched the dead and the dying of the neighborhood, and then, as soon as she had sewn her customers into that linen cloth from which they would emerge no more, she went and took up her iron to smooth out the linen of the living. Wrinkled like a last year's apple, spiteful, envious, avaricious with a phenomenal avarice, bent double, as if she had been broken in half across the loins by the constant motion of passing the iron over the linen, one might have said that she had a kind of abnormal and cynical love of a death struggle. She never spoke of anything but of the people she had seen die, of the various kinds of deaths at which she had been present, and she related with the greatest minuteness details which were always similar, just as a sportsman recounts his luck.

When Honore Bontemps entered her cottage, he found her preparing the starch for the collars of the women villagers, and he said: "Good-evening; I hope you are pretty well, Mother Rapet?"

She turned her head round to look at him, and said: "As usual, as usual, and you?" "Oh! as for me, I am as well as I could wish, but my mother is not well." "Your mother?" "Yes, my mother!" "What is the matter with her?" "She is going to turn up her toes, that's what's the matter with her!"

The old woman took her hands out of the water and asked with sudden sympathy: "Is she as bad as all that?" "The doctor says she will not last till morning." "Then she certainly is very bad!" Honore hesitated, for he wanted to make a few preparatory remarks before coming to his proposition; but as he could hit upon nothing, he made up his mind suddenly.

"How much will you ask to stay with her till the end? You know that I am not rich, and I can not even afford to keep a servant girl. It is just that which has brought my poor mother to this state—too much worry and fatigue! She did the work of ten, in spite of her ninety-two years. You don't find any made of that stuff nowadays!"

La Rapet answered gravely: "There are two prices: Forty sous by day and three francs by night for the rich, and twenty sous by day and forty by night for the others. You shall pay me the twenty and forty." But the, peasant reflected, for he knew his mother well. He knew how tenacious of life, how vigorous and unyielding she was, and she might last another week, in spite of the doctor's opinion; and so he said resolutely: "No, I would rather you would fix a price for the whole time until the end. I will take my chance, one way or the other. The doctor says she will die very soon. If that happens, so much the better for you, and so much the worse for her, but if she holds out till to-morrow or longer, so much the better for her and so much the worse for you!"

The nurse looked at the man in astonishment, for she had never treated a death as a speculation, and she hesitated, tempted by the idea of the possible gain, but she suspected that he wanted to play her a trick. "I can say nothing until I have seen your mother," she replied.

"Then come with me and see her."

She washed her hands, and went with him immediately.

They did not speak on the road; she walked with short, hasty steps, while he strode on with his long legs, as if he were crossing a brook at every step.

The cows lying down in the fields, overcome by the heat, raised their heads heavily and lowed feebly at the two passers-by, as if to ask them for some green grass.

When they got near the house, Honore Bontemps murmured: "Suppose it is all over?" And his unconscious wish that it might be so showed itself in the sound of his voice.

But the old woman was not dead. She was lying on her back, on her wretched bed, her hands covered with a purple cotton counterpane, horribly thin, knotty hands, like the claws of strange animals, like crabs, half closed by rheumatism, fatigue and the work of nearly a century which she had accomplished.

La Rapet went up to the bed and looked at the dying woman, felt her pulse, tapped her on the chest, listened to her breathing, and asked her questions, so as to hear her speak; and then, having looked at her for some time, she went out of the room, followed by Honore. Her decided opinion was that the old woman would not last till night. He asked: "Well?" And the sick-nurse replied: "Well, she may last two days, perhaps three. You will have to give me six francs, everything included."

"Six francs! six francs!" he shouted. "Are you out of your mind? I tell you she cannot last more than five or six hours!" And they disputed angrily for some time, but as the nurse said she must go home, as the time was going by, and as his wheat would not come to the farmyard of its own accord, he finally agreed to her terms.

"Very well, then, that is settled; six francs, including everything, until the corpse is taken out."

And he went away, with long strides, to his wheat which was lying on the ground under the hot sun which ripens the grain, while the sick-nurse went in again to the house.

She had brought some work with her, for she worked without ceasing by the side of the dead and dying, sometimes for herself, sometimes for the family which employed her as seamstress and paid her rather more in that capacity. Suddenly, she asked: "Have you received the last sacraments, Mother Bontemps?"

The old peasant woman shook her head, and La Rapet, who was very devout, got up quickly:

"Good heavens, is it possible? I will go and fetch the cure"; and she rushed off to the parsonage so quickly that the urchins in the street thought some accident had happened, when they saw her running.

The priest came immediately in his surplice, preceded by a choir boy who rang a bell to announce the passage of the Host through the parched and quiet country. Some men who were working at a distance took off their large hats and remained motionless until the white vestment had disappeared behind some farm buildings; the women who were making up the sheaves stood up to make the sign of the cross; the frightened black hens ran away along the ditch until they reached a well-known hole, through which they suddenly disappeared, while a foal which was tied in a meadow took fright at the sight of the surplice and began to gallop round and round, kicking cut every now and then. The acolyte, in his red cassock, walked quickly, and the priest, with his head inclined toward one shoulder and his square biretta on his head, followed him, muttering some prayers; while last of all came La Rapet, bent almost double as if she wished to prostrate herself, as she walked with folded hands as they do in church.

Honore saw them pass in the distance, and he asked: "Where is our priest going?" His man, who was more intelligent, replied: "He is taking the sacrament to your mother, of course!"

The peasant was not surprised, and said: "That may be," and went on with his work.

Mother Bontemps confessed, received absolution and communion, and the priest took his departure, leaving the two women alone in the suffocating room, while La Rapet began to look at the dying woman, and to ask herself whether it could last much longer.

The day was on the wane, and gusts of cooler air began to blow, causing a view of Epinal, which was fastened to the wall by two pins, to flap up and down; the scanty window curtains, which had formerly been white, but were now yellow and covered with fly-specks, looked as if they were going to fly off, as if they were struggling to get away, like the old woman's soul.

Lying motionless, with her eyes open, she seemed to await with indifference that death which was so near and which yet delayed its coming. Her short breathing whistled in her constricted throat. It would stop altogether soon, and there would be one woman less in the world; no one would regret her.

At nightfall Honore returned, and when he went up to the bed and saw that his mother was still alive, he asked: "How is she?" just as he had done formerly when she had been ailing, and then he sent La Rapet away, saying to her: "To-morrow morning at five o'clock, without fail." And she replied: "To-morrow, at five o'clock."

She came at daybreak, and found Honore eating his soup, which he had made himself before going to work, and the sick-nurse asked him: "Well, is your mother dead?" "She is rather better, on the contrary," he replied, with a sly look out of the corner of his eyes. And he went out.

La Rapet, seized with anxiety, went up to the dying woman, who remained in the same state, lethargic and impassive, with her eyes open and her hands clutching the counterpane. The nurse perceived that this might go on thus for two days, four days, eight days, and her avaricious mind was seized with fear, while she was furious at the sly fellow who had tricked her, and at the woman who would not die.

Nevertheless, she began to work, and waited, looking intently at the wrinkled face of Mother Bontemps. When Honore returned to breakfast he seemed quite satisfied and even in a bantering humor. He was decidedly getting in his wheat under very favorable circumstances.

La Rapet was becoming exasperated; every minute now seemed to her so much time and money stolen from her. She felt a mad inclination to take this old woman, this, headstrong old fool, this obstinate old wretch, and to stop that short, rapid breath, which was robbing her of her time and money, by squeezing her throat a little. But then she reflected on the danger of doing so, and other thoughts came into her head; so she went up to the bed and said: "Have you ever seen the Devil?" Mother Bontemps murmured: "No."

Then the sick-nurse began to talk and to tell her tales which were likely to terrify the weak mind of the dying woman. Some minutes before one dies the Devil appears, she said, to all who are in the death throes. He has a broom in his hand, a saucepan on his head, and he utters loud cries. When anybody sees him, all is over, and that person has only a few moments longer to live. She then enumerated all those to whom the Devil had appeared that year: Josephine Loisel, Eulalie Ratier, Sophie Padaknau, Seraphine Grospied.

Mother Bontemps, who had at last become disturbed in mind, moved about, wrung her hands, and tried to turn her head to look toward the end of the room. Suddenly La Rapet disappeared at the foot of the bed. She took a sheet out of the cupboard and wrapped herself up in it; she put the iron saucepan on her head, so that its three short bent feet rose up like horns, and she took a broom in her right hand and a tin pail in her left, which she threw up suddenly, so that it might fall to the ground noisily.

When it came down, it certainly made a terrible noise. Then, climbing upon a chair, the nurse lifted up the curtain which hung at the bottom of the bed, and showed herself, gesticulating and uttering shrill cries into the iron saucepan which covered her face, while she menaced the old peasant woman, who was nearly dead, with her broom.

Terrified, with an insane expression on her face, the dying woman made a superhuman effort to get up and escape; she even got her shoulders and chest out of bed; then she fell back with a deep sigh. All was over, and La Rapet calmly put everything back into its place; the broom into the corner by the cupboard the sheet inside it, the saucepan on the hearth, the pail on the floor, and the chair against the wall. Then, with professional movements, she closed the dead woman's large eyes, put a plate on the bed and poured some holy water into it, placing in it the twig of boxwood that had been nailed to the chest of drawers, and kneeling down, she fervently repeated the prayers for the dead, which she knew by heart, as a matter of business.

And when Honore returned in the evening he found her praying, and he calculated immediately that she had made twenty sows out of him, for she had only spent three days and one night there, which made five francs altogether, instead of the six which he owed her.

THE SNIPE

Old Baron des Ravots had for forty years been the champion sportsman of his province. But a stroke of paralysis had kept him in his chair for the last five or six years. He could now only shoot pigeons from the window of his drawing-room or from the top of his high doorsteps.

He spent his time in reading.

He was a good-natured business man, who had much of the literary spirit of a former century. He worshipped anecdotes, those little risque anecdotes, and also true stories of events that happened in his neighborhood. As soon as a friend came to see him he asked:

"Well, anything new?"

And he knew how to worm out information like an examining lawyer.

On sunny days he had his large reclining chair, similar to a bed, wheeled to the hall door. A man servant behind him held his guns, loaded them and handed them to his master. Another valet, hidden in the bushes, let fly a pigeon from time to time at irregular intervals, so that the baron should be unprepared and be always on the watch.

And from morning till night he fired at the birds, much annoyed if he were taken by surprise and laughing till he cried when the animal fell straight to the earth or, turned over in some comical and unexpected manner. He would turn to the man who was loading the gun and say, almost choking with laughter:

"Did that get him, Joseph? Did you see how he fell?" Joseph invariably replied:

"Oh, monsieur le baron never misses them."

In autumn, when the shooting season opened, he invited his friends as he had done formerly, and loved to hear them firing in the distance. He counted the shots and was pleased when they followed each other rapidly. And in the evening he made each guest give a faithful account of his day. They remained three hours at table telling about their sport.

They were strange and improbable adventures in which the romancing spirit of the sportsmen delighted. Some of them were memorable stories and were repeated regularly. The story of a rabbit that little Vicomte de Bourril had missed in his vestibule convulsed them with laughter each year anew. Every five minutes a fresh speaker would say:

"I heard 'birr! birr!' and a magnificent covey rose at ten paces from me. I aimed. Pif! paf! and I saw a shower, a veritable shower of birds. There were seven of them!"

And they all went into raptures, amazed, but reciprocally credulous.

But there was an old custom in the house called "The Story of the Snipe."

Whenever this queen of birds was in season the same ceremony took place at each dinner. As they worshipped this incomparable bird, each guest ate one every evening, but the heads were all left in the dish.

Then the baron, acting the part of a bishop, had a plate brought to him containing a little fat, and he carefully anointed the precious heads, holding them by the tip of their slender, needle-like beak. A lighted candle was placed beside him and everyone was silent in an anxiety of expectation.

Then he took one of the heads thus prepared, stuck a pin through it and stuck the pin on a cork, keeping the whole contrivance steady by means of little crossed sticks, and carefully placed this object on the neck of a bottle in the manner of a tourniquet.

All the guests counted simultaneously in a loud tone—
"One-two-three."

And the baron with a fillip of the finger made this toy whirl round.

The guest to whom the long beak pointed when the head stopped became the possessor of all the heads, a feast fit for a king, which made his neighbors look askance.

He took them one by one and toasted them over the candle. The grease sputtered, the roasting flesh smoked and the lucky winner ate the head, holding it by the beak and uttering exclamations of enjoyment.

And at each head the diners, raising their glasses, drank to his health.

When he had finished the last head he was obliged, at the baron's orders, to tell an anecdote to compensate the disappointed ones.

Here are some of the stories.

THE WILL

I knew that tall young fellow, Rene de Bourneval. He was an agreeable man, though rather melancholy and seemed prejudiced against everything, was very skeptical, and he could with a word tear down social hypocrisy. He would often say:

"There are no honorable men, or, at least, they are only relatively so when compared with those lower than themselves."

He had two brothers, whom he never saw, the Messieurs de Courcils. I always supposed they were by another father, on account of the difference in the name. I had frequently heard that the family had a strange history, but did not know the details. As I took a great liking to Rene we soon became intimate friends, and one evening, when I had been dining with him alone, I asked him, by chance: "Are you a son of the first or second marriage?" He grew rather pale, and then flushed, and did not speak for a few moments; he was visibly embarrassed. Then he smiled in the melancholy, gentle manner, which was peculiar to him, and said:

"My dear friend, if it will not weary you, I can give you some very strange particulars about my life. I know that you are a sensible man, so I do not fear that our friendship will suffer by my revelations; and should it suffer, I should not care about having you for my friend any longer.

"My mother, Madame de Courcils, was a poor little, timid woman, whom her husband had married for the sake of her fortune, and her whole life was one of martyrdom. Of a loving, timid, sensitive disposition, she was constantly being ill-treated by the man who ought to have been my father, one of those boors called country gentlemen. A month after their marriage he was living a licentious life and carrying on liaisons with the wives and daughters of his tenants. This did not prevent him from having three children by his wife, that is, if you count me in. My mother said nothing, and lived in that noisy house like a little mouse. Set aside, unnoticed, nervous, she looked at people with her bright, uneasy, restless eyes, the eyes of some terrified creature which can never shake off its fear. And yet she was pretty, very pretty and fair, a pale blonde, as if her hair had lost its color through her constant fear.

"Among the friends of Monsieur de Courcils who constantly came to her chateau, there was an ex-cavalry officer, a widower, a man who was feared, who was at the same time tender and violent, capable of the most determined resolves, Monsieur de Bourneval, whose name I bear. He was a tall, thin man, with a heavy black mustache. I am very like him. He was a man who had read a great deal, and his ideas were not like those of most of his class. His great-grandmother had been a friend of J. J. Rousseau's, and one might have said that he had inherited something of this ancestral connection. He knew the Contrat Social, and the Nouvelle Heloise by heart, and all those philosophical books which prepared in advance the overthrow of our old usages, prejudices, superannuated laws and imbecile morality.

"It seems that he loved my mother, and she loved him, but their liaison was carried on so secretly that no one guessed at its existence. The poor, neglected, unhappy woman must have clung to him in despair, and in her intimacy with him must have imbibed all his ways of thinking, theories of free thought, audacious ideas of independent love; but being so timid she never ventured to speak out, and it was all driven back, condensed, shut up in her heart.

"My two brothers were very hard towards her, like their father, and never gave her a caress, and, accustomed to seeing her count for nothing in the house, they treated her rather like a servant. I was the only one of her sons who really loved her and whom she loved.

"When she died I was seventeen, and I must add, in order that you may understand what follows, that a lawsuit between my father and mother had been decided in my mother's favor, giving her the bulk of the property, and, thanks to the tricks of the law, and the intelligent devotion of a lawyer to her interests, the right to make her will in favor of whom she pleased.

"We were told that there was a will at the lawyer's office and were invited to be present at the reading of it. I can remember it, as if it were yesterday. It was an imposing scene, dramatic, burlesque and surprising, occasioned by the posthumous revolt of that dead woman, by the cry for liberty, by the demands of that martyred one who had been crushed by our oppression during her lifetime and who, from her closed tomb, uttered a despairing appeal for independence.

"The man who believed he was my father, a stout, ruddy-faced man, who looked like a butcher, and my brothers, two great fellows of twenty and twenty-two, were waiting quietly in their chairs. Monsieur de Bourneval, who had been invited to be present, came in and stood behind me. He was very pale and bit his mustache, which was turning gray. No doubt he was prepared for what was going to happen. The lawyer double-locked the door and began to read the will, after having opened, in our presence, the envelope, sealed with red wax, of the contents of which he was ignorant."

My friend stopped talking abruptly, and rising, took from his writing-table an old paper, unfolded it, kissed it and then continued: "This is the will of my beloved mother:

"'I, the undersigned, Anne Catherine-Genevieve-Mathilde de Croixluce, the legitimate wife of Leopold-Joseph Gontran de Councils sound in body and mind, here express my last wishes.

"I first of all ask God, and then my dear son Rene to pardon me for the act I am about to commit. I believe that my child's heart is great enough to understand me, and to forgive me. I have suffered my whole life long. I was married out of calculation, then despised, misunderstood, oppressed and constantly deceived by my husband.

"'I forgive him, but I owe him nothing.

"'My elder sons never loved me, never petted me, scarcely treated me
as a mother, but during my whole life I did my duty towards them, and I owe them nothing more after my death. The ties of blood cannot exist without daily and constant affection. An ungrateful son is less than a stranger; he is a culprit, for he has no right to be indifferent towards his mother.*

"'I have always trembled before men, before their unjust laws, their inhuman customs, their shameful prejudices. Before God, I have no longer any fear. Dead, I fling aside disgraceful hypocrisy; I dare to speak my thoughts, and to avow and to sign the secret of my heart.*

"'I therefore leave that part of my fortune of which the law allows me to dispose, in trust to my dear lover, Pierre-Germer-Simon de Bourneval, to revert afterwards to our dear son Rene.

"'(This bequest is specified more precisely in a deed drawn up by a notary.)*

"*'And I declare before the Supreme Judge who hears me, that I should*
have cursed heaven and my own existence, if I had not found the deep, devoted, tender, unshaken affection of my lover; if I had not felt in his arms that the Creator made His creatures to love, sustain and console each other, and to weep together in the hours of sadness.

"*'Monsieur de Courcils is the father of my two eldest sons; Rene, alone, owes his life to Monsieur de Bourneval. I pray the Master of men and of their destinies, to place father and son above social prejudices, to make them love each other until they die, and to love me also in my coffin.*

"*'These are my last thoughts, and my last wish.*

"'MATHILDE DE CROIXLUCE.'"

"Monsieur de Courcils had risen and he cried:

"'It is the will of a madwoman.'

"Then Monsieur de Bourneval stepped forward and said in a loud, penetrating voice: 'I, Simon de Bourneval, solemnly declare that this writing contains nothing but the strict truth, and I am ready to prove it by letters which I possess.'

"On hearing that, Monsieur de Courcils went up to him, and I thought that they were going to attack each other. There they stood, both of them tall, one stout and the other thin, both trembling. My mother's husband stammered out: 'You are a worthless wretch!' And the other replied in a loud, dry voice: 'We will meet elsewhere, monsieur. I should have already slapped your ugly face and challenged you long since if I had not, before everything else, thought of the peace of mind during her lifetime of that poor woman whom you caused to suffer so greatly.'

"Then, turning to me, he said: 'You are my son; will you come with me? I have no right to take you away, but I shall assume it, if you are willing to come with me: I shook his hand without replying, and we went out together. I was certainly three parts mad.

"Two days later Monsieur de Bourneval killed Monsieur de Courcils in a duel. My brothers, to avoid a terrible scandal, held their tongues. I offered them and they accepted half the fortune which my mother had left me. I took my real father's name, renouncing that which the law gave me, but which was not really mine. Monsieur de Bourneval died three years later and I am still inconsolable."

He rose from his chair, walked up and down the room, and, standing in front of me, said:

"Well, I say that my mother's will was one of the most beautiful, the most loyal, as well as one of the grandest acts that a woman could perform. Do you not think so?"

I held out both hands to him, saying:

"I most certainly do, my friend."

WALTER SCHNAFFS' ADVENTURE

*E*ver since he entered France with the invading army Walter Schnaffs had considered himself the most unfortunate of men. He was large, had difficulty in walking, was short of breath and suffered frightfully with his feet, which were very flat and very fat. But he was a peaceful, benevolent man, not warlike or sanguinary, the father of four children whom he adored, and married to a little blonde whose little tendernesses, attentions and kisses he recalled with despair every evening. He liked to rise late and retire early, to eat good things in a leisurely manner and to drink beer in the saloon. He reflected, besides, that all that is sweet in existence vanishes with life, and he maintained in his heart a fearful hatred, instinctive as well as logical, for cannon, rifles, revolvers and swords, but especially for bayonets, feeling that he was unable to dodge this dangerous weapon rapidly enough to protect his big paunch.

And when night fell and he lay on the ground, wrapped in his cape beside his comrades who were snoring, he thought long and deeply about those he had left behind and of the dangers in his path. "If he were killed what would become of the little ones? Who would provide for them and bring them up?" Just at present they were not rich, although he had borrowed when he left so as to leave them some money. And Walter Schnaffs wept when he thought of all this.

At the beginning of a battle his legs became so weak that he would have fallen if he had not reflected that the entire army would pass over his body. The whistling of the bullets gave him gooseflesh.

For months he had lived thus in terror and anguish.

His company was marching on Normandy, and one day he was sent to reconnoitre with a small detachment, simply to explore a portion of the territory and to return at once. All seemed quiet in the country; nothing indicated an armed resistance.

But as the Prussians were quietly descending into a little valley traversed by deep ravines a sharp fusillade made them halt suddenly, killing twenty of their men, and a company of sharpshooters, suddenly emerging from a little wood as large as your hand, darted forward with bayonets at the end of their rifles.

Walter Schnaffs remained motionless at first, so surprised and bewildered that he did not even think of making his escape. Then he was seized with a wild desire to run away, but he remembered at once that he ran like a tortoise compared with those thin Frenchmen, who came bounding along like a lot of goats. Perceiving a large ditch full of brushwood covered with dead leaves about six paces in front of him, he sprang into it with both feet together, without stopping to think of its depth, just as one jumps from a bridge into the river.

He fell like an arrow through a thick layer of vines and thorny brambles that tore his face and hands and landed heavily in a sitting posture on a bed of stones. Raising his eyes, he saw the sky through the hole he had made in falling through. This aperture might betray him, and he crawled along carefully on hands and knees at the bottom of this ditch beneath the covering of interlacing branches, going as fast as he could and getting away from the scene of the skirmish. Presently he stopped and sat down, crouched like a hare amid the tall dry grass.

He heard firing and cries and groans going on for some time. Then the noise of fighting grew fainter and ceased. All was quiet and silent.

Suddenly something stirred, beside him. He was frightfully startled. It was a little bird which had perched on a branch and was moving the dead leaves. For almost an hour Walter Schnaffs' heart beat loud and rapidly.

Night fell, filling the ravine with its shadows. The soldier began to think. What was he to do? What was to become of him? Should he rejoin the army? But how? By what road? And he began over again the horrible life of anguish, of terror, of fatigue and suffering that he had led since the commencement of the war. No! He no longer had the courage! He would not have the energy necessary to endure long marches and to face the dangers to which one was exposed at every moment.

But what should he do? He could not stay in this ravine in concealment until the end of hostilities. No, indeed! If it were not for having to eat, this prospect would not have daunted him greatly. But he had to eat, to eat every day.

And here he was, alone, armed and in uniform, on the enemy's territory, far from those who would protect him. A shiver ran over him.

All at once he thought: "If I were only a prisoner!" And his heart quivered with a longing, an intense desire to be taken prisoner by the French. A prisoner, he would be saved, fed, housed, sheltered from bullets and swords, without any apprehension whatever, in a good, well-kept prison. A prisoner! What a dream:

His resolution was formed at once.

"I will constitute myself a prisoner."

He rose, determined to put this plan into execution without a moment's delay. But he stood motionless, suddenly a prey to disturbing reflections and fresh terrors.

Where would he make himself a prisoner and how? In What direction? And frightful pictures, pictures of death came into his mind.

He would run terrible danger in venturing alone through the country with his pointed helmet.

Supposing he should meet some peasants. These peasants seeing a Prussian who had lost his way, an unprotected Prussian, would kill him as if he were a stray dog! They would murder him with their forks, their picks, their scythes and their shovels. They would make a stew of him, a pie, with the frenzy of exasperated, conquered enemies.

If he should meet the sharpshooters! These sharpshooters, madmen without law or discipline, would shoot him just for amusement to pass an hour; it would make them laugh to see his head. And he fancied he was already leaning against a wall in-front of four rifles whose little black apertures seemed to be gazing at him.

Supposing he should meet the French army itself. The vanguard would take him for a scout, for some bold and sly trooper who had set off alone to reconnoitre, and they would fire at him. And he could already hear, in imagination, the irregular shots of soldiers lying in the brush, while he himself, standing in the middle of the field, was sinking to the earth, riddled like a sieve with bullets which he felt piercing his flesh.

He sat down again in despair. His situation seemed hopeless.

It was quite a dark, black and silent night. He no longer budged, trembling at all the slight and unfamiliar sounds that occur at night. The sound of a rabbit crouching at the edge of his burrow almost made him run. The cry of an owl caused him positive anguish, giving him a nervous shock that pained like a wound. He opened his big eyes as wide as possible to try and see through the darkness, and he imagined every moment that he heard someone walking close beside him.

After interminable hours in which he suffered the tortures of the damned, he noticed through his leafy cover that the sky was becoming bright. He at once felt an intense relief. His limbs stretched out, suddenly relaxed, his heart quieted down, his eyes closed; he fell asleep.

When he awoke the sun appeared to be almost at the meridian. It must be noon. No sound disturbed the gloomy silence. Walter Schnaffs noticed that he was exceedingly hungry.

He yawned, his mouth watering at the thought of sausage, the good sausage the soldiers have, and he felt a gnawing at his stomach.

He rose from the ground, walked a few steps, found that his legs were weak and sat down to reflect. For two or three hours he again considered the pros and cons, changing his mind every moment, baffled, unhappy, torn by the most conflicting motives.

Finally he had an idea that seemed logical and practical. It was to watch for a villager passing by alone, unarmed and with no dangerous tools of his trade, and to run to him and give himself up, making him understand that he was surrendering.

He took off his helmet, the point of which might betray him, and put his head out of his hiding place with the utmost caution.

No solitary pedestrian could be perceived on the horizon. Yonder, to the right, smoke rose from the chimney of a little village, smoke from kitchen fires! And yonder, to the left, he saw at the end of an avenue of trees a large turreted chateau. He waited till evening, suffering frightfully from hunger, seeing nothing but flights of crows, hearing nothing but the silent expostulation of his empty stomach.

And darkness once more fell on him.

He stretched himself out in his retreat and slept a feverish sleep, haunted by nightmares, the sleep of a starving man.

Dawn again broke above his head and he began to make his observations. But the landscape was deserted as on the previous day, and a new fear came into Walter Schnaffs' mind—the fear of death by hunger! He pictured himself lying at full length on his back at the bottom of his hiding place, with his two eyes closed, and animals, little creatures of all kinds, approached and began to feed on his dead body, attacking it all over at once, gliding beneath his clothing to bite his cold flesh, and a big crow pecked out his eyes with its sharp beak.

He almost became crazy, thinking he was going to faint and would not be able to walk. And he was just preparing to rush off to the village, determined to dare anything, to brave everything, when he perceived three peasants walking to the fields with their forks across their shoulders, and he dived back into his hiding place.

But as soon as it grew dark he slowly emerged from the ditch and started off, stooping and fearful, with beating heart, towards the distant chateau, preferring to go there rather than to the village, which seemed to him as formidable as a den of tigers.

The lower windows were brilliantly lighted. One of them was open and from it escaped a strong odor of roast meat, an odor which suddenly penetrated to the olfactories and to the stomach of Walter Schnaffs, tickling his nerves, making him breathe quickly, attracting him irresistibly and inspiring his heart with the boldness of desperation.

And abruptly, without reflection, he placed himself, helmet on head, in front of the window.

Eight servants were at dinner around a large table. But suddenly one of the maids sat there, her mouth agape, her eyes fixed and letting fall her glass. They all followed the direction of her gaze.

They saw the enemy!

Good God! The Prussians were attacking the chateau!

There was a shriek, only one shriek made up of eight shrieks uttered in eight different keys, a terrific screaming of terror, then a tumultuous rising from their seats, a jostling, a scrimmage and a wild rush to the door at the farther end. Chairs fell over, the men knocked the women down and walked over them. In two seconds the room was empty, deserted, and the table, covered with eatables, stood in front of Walter Schnaffs, lost in amazement and still standing at the window.

After some moments of hesitation he climbed in at the window and approached the table. His fierce hunger caused him to tremble as if he were in a fever, but fear still held him back, numbed him. He listened. The entire house seemed to shudder. Doors closed, quick steps ran along the floor above. The uneasy Prussian listened eagerly to these confused sounds. Then he heard dull sounds, as though bodies were falling to the ground at the foot of the walls, human beings jumping from the first floor.

Then all motion, all disturbance ceased, and the great chateau became as silent as the grave.

Walter Schnaffs sat down before a clean plate and began to eat. He took great mouthfuls, as if he feared he might be interrupted before he had swallowed enough. He shovelled the food into his mouth, open like a trap, with both hands, and chunks of food went into his stomach, swelling out his throat as it passed down.

Now and then he stopped, almost ready to burst like a stopped-up pipe. Then he would take the cider jug and wash down his esophagus as one washes out a clogged rain pipe.

He emptied all the plates, all the dishes and all the bottles. Then, intoxicated with drink and food, besotted, red in the face, shaken by hiccoughs, his mind clouded and his speech thick, he unbuttoned his uniform in order to breathe or he could not have taken a step. His eyes closed, his mind became torpid; he leaned his heavy forehead on his folded arms on the table and gradually lost all consciousness of things and events.

The last quarter of the moon above the trees in the park shed a faint light on the landscape. It was the chill hour that precedes the dawn.

Numerous silent shadows glided among the trees and occasionally a blade of steel gleamed in the shadow as a ray of moonlight struck it.

The quiet chateau stood there in dark outline. Only two windows were still lighted up on the ground floor.

Suddenly a voice thundered:

"Forward! nom d'un nom! To the breach, my lads!"

And in an instant the doors, shutters and window panes fell in beneath a wave of men who rushed in, breaking, destroying everything, and took the house by storm. In a moment fifty soldiers, armed to the teeth, bounded into the kitchen, where Walter Schnaffs was peacefully sleeping, and placing to his breast fifty loaded rifles, they overturned him, rolled him on the floor, seized him and tied his head and feet together.

He gasped in amazement, too besotted to understand, perplexed, bruised and wild with fear.

Suddenly a big soldier, covered with gold lace, put his foot on his stomach, shouting:

"You are my prisoner. Surrender!"

The Prussian heard only the one word "prisoner" and he sighed, "Ya, ya, ya."

He was raised from the floor, tied in a chair and examined with lively curiosity by his victors, who were blowing like whales. Several of them sat down, done up with excitement and fatigue.

He smiled, actually smiled, secure now that he was at last a prisoner.

Another officer came into the room and said:

"Colonel, the enemy has escaped; several seem to have been wounded. We are in possession."

The big officer, who was wiping his forehead, exclaimed: "Victory!"

And he wrote in a little business memorandum book which he took from his pocket:

"After a desperate encounter the Prussians were obliged to beat a retreat, carrying with them their dead and wounded, the number of whom is estimated at fifty men. Several were taken prisoners."

The young officer inquired:

"What steps shall I take, colonel?"

"We will retire in good order," replied the colonel, "to avoid having to return and make another attack with artillery and a larger force of men."

And he gave the command to set out.

The column drew up in line in the darkness beneath the walls of the chateau and filed out, a guard of six soldiers with revolvers in their hands surrounding Walter Schnaffs, who was firmly bound.

Scouts were sent ahead to reconnoitre. They advanced cautiously, halting from time to time.

At daybreak they arrived at the district of La Roche-Oysel, whose national guard had accomplished this feat of arms.

The uneasy and excited inhabitants were expecting them. When they saw the prisoner's helmet tremendous shouts arose. The women raised their arms in wonder, the old people wept. An old grandfather threw his crutch at the Prussian and struck the nose of one of their own defenders.

The colonel roared:

"See that the prisoner is secure!"

At length they reached the town hall. The prison was opened and Walter Schnaffs, freed from his bonds, cast into it. Two hundred armed men mounted guard outside the building.

Then, in spite of the indigestion that had been troubling him for some time, the Prussian, wild with joy, began to dance about, to dance frantically, throwing out his arms and legs and uttering wild shouts until he fell down exhausted beside the wall.

He was a prisoner-saved!

That was how the Chateau de Charnpignet was taken from the enemy after only six hours of occupation.

Colonel Ratier, a cloth merchant, who had led the assault at the head of a body of the national guard of La Roche-Oysel, was decorated with an order.

AT SEA

$\mathcal{T}$he following paragraphs recently appeared in the papers:
  "Boulogne-Sur-Mer, January 22.—Our correspondent writes:

"A fearful accident has thrown our sea-faring population, which has suffered so much in the last two years, into the greatest consternation. The fishing smack commanded by Captain Javel, on entering the harbor was wrecked on the rocks of the harbor breakwater.

"In spite of the efforts of the life boat and the shooting of life lines from the shore four sailors and the cabin boy were lost.

"The rough weather continues. Fresh disasters are anticipated."

Who is this Captain Javel? Is he the brother of the one-armed man?

If the poor man tossed about in the waves and dead, perhaps, beneath his wrecked boat, is the one I am thinking of, he took part, just eighteen years ago, in another tragedy, terrible and simple as are all these fearful tragedies of the sea.

Javel, senior, was then master of a trawling smack.

The trawling smack is the ideal fishing boat. So solidly built that it fears no weather, with a round bottom, tossed about unceasingly on the waves like a cork, always on top, always thrashed by the harsh salt winds of the English Channel, it ploughs the sea unweariedly with bellying sail, dragging along at its side a huge trawling net, which scours the depths of the ocean, and detaches and gathers in all the animals asleep in the rocks, the flat fish glued to the sand, the heavy crabs with their curved claws, and the lobsters with their pointed mustaches.

When the breeze is fresh and the sea choppy, the boat starts in to trawl. The net is fastened all along a big log of wood clamped with iron and is let down by two ropes on pulleys at either end of the boat. And the boat, driven by the wind and the tide, draws along this apparatus which ransacks and plunders the depths of the sea.

Javel had on board his younger brother, four sailors and a cabin boy. He had set sail from Boulogne on a beautiful day to go trawling.

But presently a wind sprang up, and a hurricane obliged the smack to run to shore. She gained the English coast, but the high sea broke against the rocks and dashed on the beach, making it impossible to go into port, filling all the harbor entrances with foam and noise and danger.

The smack started off again, riding on the waves, tossed, shaken, dripping, buffeted by masses of water, but game in spite of everything; accustomed to this boisterous weather, which sometimes kept it roving between the two neighboring countries without its being able to make port in either.

At length the hurricane calmed down just as they were in the open, and although the sea was still high the captain gave orders to cast the net.

So it was lifted overboard, and two men in the bows and two in the stern began to unwind the ropes that held it. It suddenly touched bottom, but a big wave made the boat heel, and Javel, junior, who was in the bows directing the lowering of the net, staggered, and his arm was caught in the rope which the shock had slipped from the pulley for an instant. He made a desperate effort to raise the rope with the other hand, but the net was down and the taut rope did not give.

The man cried out in agony. They all ran to his aid. His brother left the rudder. They all seized the rope, trying to free the arm it was bruising. But in vain. "We must cut it," said a sailor, and he took from his pocket a big knife, which, with two strokes, could save young Javel's arm.

But if the rope were cut the trawling net would be lost, and this net was worth money, a great deal of money, fifteen hundred francs. And it belonged to Javel, senior, who was tenacious of his property.

"No, do not cut, wait, I will luff," he cried, in great distress. And he ran to the helm and turned the rudder. But the boat scarcely obeyed it, being impeded by the net which kept it from going forward, and prevented also by the force of the tide and the wind.

Javel, junior, had sunk on his knees, his teeth clenched, his eyes haggard. He did not utter a word. His brother came back to him, in dread of the sailor's knife.

"Wait, wait," he said. "We will let down the anchor."

They cast anchor, and then began to turn the capstan to loosen the moorings of the net. They loosened them at length and disengaged the imprisoned arm, in its bloody woolen sleeve.

Young Javel seemed like an idiot. They took off his jersey and saw a horrible sight, a mass of flesh from which the blood spurted as if from a pump. Then the young man looked at his arm and murmured: "Foutu" (done for).

Then, as the blood was making a pool on the deck of the boat, one of the sailors cried: "He will bleed to death, we must bind the vein."

So they took a cord, a thick, brown, tarry cord, and twisting it around the arm above the wound, tightened it with all their might. The blood ceased to spurt by slow degrees, and, presently, stopped altogether.

Young Javel rose, his arm hanging at his side. He took hold of it with the other hand, raised it, turned it over, shook it. It was all mashed, the bones broken, the muscles alone holding it together. He looked at it sadly, reflectively. Then he sat down on a folded sail and his comrades advised him to keep wetting the arm constantly to prevent it from mortifying.

They placed a pail of water beside him, and every few minutes he dipped a glass into it and bathed the frightful wound, letting the clear water trickle on to it.

"You would be better in the cabin," said his brother. He went down, but came up again in an hour, not caring to be alone. And, besides, he preferred the fresh air. He sat down again on his sail and began to bathe his arm.

They made a good haul. The broad fish with their white bellies lay beside him, quivering in the throes of death; he looked at them as he continued to bathe his crushed flesh.

As they were about to return to Boulogne the wind sprang up anew, and the little boat resumed its mad course, bounding and tumbling about, shaking up the poor wounded man.

Night came on. The sea ran high until dawn. As the sun rose the English coast was again visible, but, as the weather had abated a little, they turned back towards the French coast, tacking as they went.

Towards evening Javel, junior, called his comrades and showed them some black spots, all the horrible tokens of mortification in the portion of the arm below the broken bones.

The sailors examined it, giving their opinion.

"That might be the 'Black,'" thought one.

"He should put salt water on it," said another.

They brought some salt water and poured it on the wound. The injured man became livid, ground his teeth and writhed a little, but did not exclaim.

Then, as soon as the smarting had abated, he said to his brother:
"Give me your knife."

The brother handed it to him.

"Hold my arm up, quite straight, and pull it."

They did as he asked them.

Then he began to cut off his arm. He cut gently, carefully, severing all the tendons with this blade that was sharp as a razor. And, presently, there was only a stump left. He gave a deep sigh and said:

"It had to be done. It was done for."

He seemed relieved and breathed loud. He then began again to pour water on the stump of arm that remained.

The sea was still rough and they could not make the shore.

When the day broke, Javel, junior, took the severed portion of his arm and examined it for a long time. Gangrene had set in. His comrades also examined it and handed it from one to the other, feeling it, turning it over, and sniffing at it.

"You must throw that into the sea at once," said his brother.

But Javel, junior, got angry.

"Oh, no! Oh, no! I don't want to. It belongs to me, does it not, as it is my arm?"

And he took and placed it between his feet.

"It will putrefy, just the same," said the older brother. Then an idea came to the injured man. In order to preserve the fish when the boat was long at sea, they packed it in salt, in barrels. He asked:

"Why can I not put it in pickle?"

"Why, that's a fact," exclaimed the others.

Then they emptied one of the barrels, which was full from the haul of the last few days; and right at the bottom of the barrel they laid the detached arm. They covered it with salt, and then put back the fish one by one.

One of the sailors said by way of joke:

"I hope we do not sell it at auction."

And everyone laughed, except the two Javels.

The wind was still boisterous. They tacked within sight of Boulogne until the following morning at ten o'clock. Young Javel continued to bathe his wound. From time to time he rose and walked from one end to the other of the boat.

His brother, who was at the tiller, followed him with glances, and shook his head.

At last they ran into harbor.

The doctor examined the wound and pronounced it to be in

good condition. He dressed it properly and ordered the patient to rest. But Javel would not go to bed until he got back his severed arm, and he returned at once to the dock to look for the barrel which he had marked with a cross.

It was emptied before him and he seized the arm, which was well preserved in the pickle, had shrunk and was freshened. He wrapped it up in a towel he had brought for the purpose and took it home.

His wife and children looked for a long time at this fragment of their father, feeling the fingers, and removing the grains of salt that were under the nails. Then they sent for a carpenter to make a little coffin.

The next day the entire crew of the trawling smack followed the funeral of the detached arm. The two brothers, side by side, led the procession; the parish beadle carried the corpse under his arm.

Javel, junior, gave up the sea. He obtained a small position on the dock, and when he subsequently talked about his accident, he would say confidentially to his auditors:

"If my brother had been willing to cut away the net, I should still have my arm, that is sure. But he was thinking only of his property."

MINUET

Great misfortunes do not affect me very much, said John Bridelle, an old bachelor who passed for a sceptic. I have seen war at quite close quarters; I walked across corpses without any feeling of pity. The great brutal facts of nature, or of humanity, may call forth cries of horror or indignation, but do not cause us that tightening of the heart, that shudder that goes down your spine at sight of certain little heartrending episodes.

The greatest sorrow that anyone can experience is certainly the loss of a child, to a mother; and the loss of his mother, to a man. It is intense, terrible, it rends your heart and upsets your mind; but one is healed of these shocks, just as large bleeding wounds become healed. Certain meetings, certain things half perceived, or surmised, certain secret sorrows, certain tricks of fate which awake in us a whole world of painful thoughts, which suddenly unclose to us the mysterious door of moral suffering, complicated, incurable; all the deeper because they appear benign, all the more bitter because they are intangible, all the more tenacious because they appear almost factitious, leave in our souls a sort of trail of sadness, a taste of bitterness, a feeling of disenchantment, from which it takes a long time to free ourselves.

I have always present to my mind two or three things that others would surely not have noticed, but which penetrated my being like fine, sharp incurable stings.

You might not perhaps understand the emotion that I retained from these hasty impressions. I will tell you one of them. She was very old, but as lively as a young girl. It may be that my imagination alone is responsible for my emotion.

I am fifty. I was young then and studying law. I was rather sad, somewhat of a dreamer, full of a pessimistic philosophy and did not care much for noisy cafes, boisterous companions, or stupid girls. I rose early and one of my chief enjoyments was to walk alone about eight o'clock in the morning in the nursery garden of the Luxembourg.

You people never knew that nursery garden. It was like a forgotten garden of the last century, as pretty as the gentle smile of an old lady. Thick hedges divided the narrow regular paths,—peaceful paths between two walls of carefully trimmed foliage. The gardener's great shears were pruning unceasingly these leafy partitions, and here and there one came across beds of flowers, lines of little trees looking like schoolboys out for a walk, companies of magnificent rose bushes, or regiments of fruit trees.

An entire corner of this charming spot was in habited by bees. Their straw hives skillfully arranged at distances on boards had their entrances—as large as the opening of a thimble—turned towards the sun, and all along the paths one encountered these humming and gilded flies, the true masters of this peaceful spot, the real promenaders of these quiet paths.

I came there almost every morning. I sat down on a bench and read. Sometimes I let my book fall on my knees, to dream, to listen to the life of Paris around me, and to enjoy the infinite repose of these old-fashioned hedges.

But I soon perceived that I was not the only one to frequent this spot as soon as the gates were opened, and I occasionally met face to face, at a turn in the path, a strange little old man.

He wore shoes with silver buckles, knee-breeches, a snuff-colored frock coat, a lace jabot, and an outlandish gray hat with wide brim and long-haired surface that might have come out of the ark.

He was thin, very thin, angular, grimacing and smiling. His bright eyes were restless beneath his eyelids which blinked continuously. He always carried in his hand a superb cane with a gold knob, which must have been for him some glorious souvenir.

This good man astonished me at first, then caused me the intensest interest. I watched him through the leafy walls, I followed him at a distance, stopping at a turn in the hedge so as not to be seen.

And one morning when he thought he was quite alone, he began to make the most remarkable motions. First he would give some little springs, then make a bow; then, with his slim legs, he would give a lively spring in the air, clapping his feet as he did so, and then turn round cleverly, skipping and frisking about in a comical manner, smiling as if he had an audience, twisting his poor little puppet-like body, bowing pathetic and ridiculous little greetings into the empty air. He was dancing.

I stood petrified with amazement, asking myself which of us was crazy, he or I.

He stopped suddenly, advanced as actors do on the stage, then bowed and retreated with gracious smiles, and kissing his hand as actors do, his trembling hand, to the two rows of trimmed bushes.

Then he continued his walk with a solemn demeanor.

After that I never lost sight of him, and each morning he began anew his outlandish exercises.

I was wildly anxious to speak to him. I decided to risk it, and one day, after greeting him, I said:

"It is a beautiful day, monsieur."

He bowed.

"Yes, sir, the weather is just as it used to be."

A week later we were friends and I knew his history. He had been a dancing master at the opera, in the time of Louis XV. His beautiful cane was a present from the Comte de Clermont. And when we spoke about dancing he never stopping talking.

One day he said to me:

"I married La Castris, monsieur. I will introduce you to her if you wish it, but she does not get here till later. This garden, you see, is our delight and our life. It is all that remains of former days. It seems as though we could not exist if we did not have it. It is old and distingue, is it not? I seem to breathe an air here that has not changed since I was young. My wife and I pass all our afternoons here, but I come in the morning because I get up early."

As soon as I had finished luncheon I returned to the Luxembourg, and presently perceived my friend offering his arm ceremoniously to a very old little lady dressed in black, to whom he introduced me. It was La Castris, the great dancer, beloved by princes, beloved by the king, beloved by all that century of gallantry that seems to have left behind it in the world an atmosphere of love.

We sat down on a bench. It was the month of May. An odor of flowers floated in the neat paths; a hot sun glided its rays between the branches and covered us with patches of light. The black dress of La Castris seemed to be saturated with sunlight.

The garden was empty. We heard the rattling of vehicles in the distance.

"Tell me," I said to the old dancer, "what was the minuet?"

He gave a start.

"The minuet, monsieur, is the queen of dances, and the dance of queens, do you understand? Since there is no longer any royalty, there is no longer any minuet."

And he began in a pompous manner a long dithyrambic eulogy which I could not understand. I wanted to have the steps, the movements, the positions, explained to me. He became confused, was amazed at his inability to make me understand, became nervous and worried.

Then suddenly, turning to his old companion who had remained silent and serious, he said:

"Elise, would you like—say—would you like, it would be very nice of you, would you like to show this gentleman what it was?"

She turned eyes uneasily in all directions, then rose without saying a word and took her position opposite him.

Then I witnessed an unheard-of thing.

They advanced and retreated with childlike grimaces, smiling, swinging each other, bowing, skipping about like two automaton dolls moved by some old mechanical contrivance, somewhat damaged, but made by a clever workman according to the fashion of his time.

And I looked at them, my heart filled with extraordinary emotions, my soul touched with an indescribable melancholy. I seemed to see before me a pathetic and comical apparition, the out-of-date ghost of a former century.

They suddenly stopped. They had finished all the figures of the dance. For some seconds they stood opposite each other, smiling in an astonishing manner. Then they fell on each other's necks sobbing.

I left for the provinces three days later. I never saw them again. When I returned to Paris, two years later, the nursery had been destroyed. What became of them, deprived of the dear garden of former days, with its mazes, its odor of the past, and the graceful windings of its hedges?

Are they dead? Are they wandering among modern streets like hopeless exiles? Are they dancing—grotesque spectres—a fantastic minuet in the moonlight, amid the cypresses of a cemetery, along the pathways bordered by graves?

Their memory haunts me, obsesses me, torments me, remains with me like a wound. Why? I do not know.

No doubt you think that very absurd?

THE SON

The two old friends were walking in the garden in bloom, where spring was bringing everything to life.

One was a senator, the other a member of the French Academy, both serious men, full of very logical but solemn arguments, men of note and reputation.

They talked first of politics, exchanging opinions; not on ideas, but on men, personalities in this regard taking the predominance over ability. Then they recalled some memories. Then they walked along in silence, enervated by the warmth of the air.

A large bed of wallflowers breathed out a delicate sweetness. A mass of flowers of all species and color flung their fragrance to the breeze, while a cytisus covered with yellow clusters scattered its fine pollen abroad, a golden cloud, with an odor of honey that bore its balmy seed across space, similar to the sachet-powders of perfumers.

The senator stopped, breathed in the cloud of floating pollen, looked at the fertile shrub, yellow as the sun, whose seed was floating in the air, and said:

"When one considers that these imperceptible fragrant atoms will create existences at a hundred leagues from here, will send a thrill through the fibres and sap of female trees and produce beings with roots, growing from a germ, just as we do, mortal like ourselves, and who will be replaced by other beings of the same order, like ourselves again!"

And, standing in front of the brilliant cytisus, whose live pollen was shaken off by each breath of air, the senator added:

"Ah, old fellow, if you had to keep count of all your children you would be mightily embarrassed. Here is one who generates freely, and then lets them go without a pang and troubles himself no more about them."

"We do the same, my friend," said the academician.

"Yes, I do not deny it; we let them go sometimes," resumed the senator, "but we are aware that we do, and that constitutes our superiority."

"No, that is not what I mean," said the other, shaking his head. "You see, my friend, that there is scarcely a man who has not some children that he does not know, children—'father unknown'—whom he has generated almost unconsciously, just as this tree reproduces.

"If we had to keep account of our amours, we should be just as embarrassed as this cytisus which you apostrophized would be in counting up his descendants, should we not?

"From eighteen to forty years, in fact, counting in every chance cursory acquaintanceship, we may well say that we have been intimate with two or three hundred women.

"Well, then, my friend, among this number can you be sure that you have not had children by at least one of them, and that you have not in the streets, or in the bagnio, some blackguard of a son who steals from and murders decent people, i.e., ourselves; or else a daughter in some disreputable place, or, if she has the good fortune to be deserted by her mother, as cook in some family?

"Consider, also, that almost all those whom we call 'prostitutes' have one or two children of whose paternal parentage they are ignorant, generated by chance at the price of ten or twenty francs. In every business there is profit and loss. These wildings constitute the 'loss' in their profession. Who generated them? You—I—we all did, the men called 'gentlemen'! They are the consequences of our jovial little dinners, of our gay evenings, of those hours when our comfortable physical being impels us to chance liaisons.

"Thieves, marauders, all these wretches, in fact, are our children. And that is better for us than if we were their children, for those scoundrels generate also!

"I have in my mind a very horrible story that I will relate to you. It has caused me incessant remorse, and, further than that, a continual doubt, a disquieting uncertainty, that, at times, torments me frightfully.

"When I was twenty-five I undertook a walking tour through Brittany with one of my friends, now a member of the cabinet.

"After walking steadily for fifteen or twenty days and visiting the Cotes-du-Nord and part of Finistere we reached Douarnenez. From there we went without halting to the wild promontory of Raz by the bay of Les Trepaases, and passed the night in a village whose name ends in 'of.' The next morning a strange lassitude kept my friend in bed; I say bed from habit, for our couch consisted simply of two bundles of straw.

"It would never do to be ill in this place. So I made him get up, and we reached Andierne about four or five o'clock in the evening.

"The following day he felt a little better, and we set out again. But on the road he was seized with intolerable pain, and we could scarcely get as far as Pont Labbe.

"Here, at least, there was an inn. My friend went to bed, and the doctor, who had been sent for from Quimper, announced that he had a high fever, without being able to determine its nature.

"Do you know Pont Labbe? No? Well, then, it is the most Breton of all this Breton Brittany, which extends from the promontory of Raz to the Morbihan, of this land which contains the essence of the Breton manners, legends and customs. Even to-day this corner of the country has scarcely changed. I say 'even to-day,' for I now go there every year, alas!

"An old chateau laves the walls of its towers in a great melancholy pond, melancholy and frequented by flights of wild birds. It has an outlet in a river on which boats can navigate as far as the town. In the narrow streets with their old-time houses the men wear big hats, embroidered waistcoats and four coats, one on top of the other; the inside one, as large as your hand, barely covering the shoulder-blades, and the outside one coming to just above the seat of the trousers.

"The girls, tall, handsome and fresh have their bosoms crushed in a cloth bodice which makes an armor, compresses them, not allowing one even to guess at their robust and tortured neck. They also wear a strange headdress. On their temples two bands embroidered in colors frame their face, inclosing the hair, which falls in a shower at the back of their heads, and is then turned up and gathered on top of the head under a singular cap, often woven with gold or silver thread.

"The servant at our inn was eighteen at most, with very blue eyes, a pale blue with two tiny black pupils, short teeth close together, which she showed continually when she laughed, and which seemed strong enough to grind granite.

"She did not know a word of French, speaking only Breton, as did most of her companions.

"As my friend did not improve much, and although he had no definite malady, the doctor forbade him to continue his journey yet, ordering complete rest. I spent my days with him, and the little maid would come in incessantly, bringing either my dinner or some herb tea.

"I teased her a little, which seemed to amuse her, but we did not chat, of course, as we could not understand each other.

"But one night, after I had stayed quite late with my friend and was going back to my room, I passed the girl, who was going to her room. It was just opposite my open door, and, without reflection, and more for fun than anything else, I abruptly seized her round the waist, and before she recovered from her astonishment I had thrown her down and locked her in my room. She looked at me, amazed, excited, terrified, not daring to cry out for fear of a scandal and of being probably driven out, first by her employers and then, perhaps, by her father.

"I did it as a joke at first. She defended herself bravely, and at the first chance she ran to the door, drew back the bolt and fled.

"I scarcely saw her for several days. She would not let me come near her. But when my friend was cured and we were to get out on our travels again I saw her coming into my room about midnight the night before our departure, just after I had retired.

"She threw herself into my arms and embraced me passionately, giving me all the assurances of tenderness and despair that a woman can give when she does not know a word of our language.

"A week later I had forgotten this adventure, so common and frequent when one is travelling, the inn servants being generally destined to amuse travellers in this way.

"I was thirty before I thought of it again, or returned to Pont Labbe.

"But in 1876 I revisited it by chance during a trip into Brittany, which I made in order to look up some data for a book and to become permeated with the atmosphere of the different places.

"Nothing seemed changed. The chateau still laved its gray wall in the pond outside the little town; the inn was the same, though it had been repaired, renovated and looked more modern. As I entered it I was received by two young Breton girls of eighteen, fresh and pretty, bound up in their tight cloth bodices, with their silver caps and wide embroidered bands on their ears.

"It was about six o'clock in the evening. I sat down to dinner, and as the host was assiduous in waiting on me himself, fate, no doubt, impelled me to say:

"'Did you know the former proprietors of this house? I spent about ten days here thirty years ago. I am talking old times.'

"'Those were my parents, monsieur,' he replied.

"Then I told him why we had stayed over at that time, how my comrade had been delayed by illness. He did not let me finish.

"'Oh, I recollect perfectly. I was about fifteen or sixteen. You slept in the room at the end and your friend in the one I have taken for myself, overlooking the street.'

"It was only then that the recollection of the little maid came vividly to my mind. I asked: 'Do you remember a pretty little servant who was then in your father's employ, and who had, if my memory does not deceive me, pretty eyes and fresh-looking teeth?'

"'Yes, monsieur; she died in childbirth some time after.'

"And, pointing to the courtyard where a thin, lame man was stirring up the manure, he added:

"'That is her son.'

"I began to laugh:

"'He is not handsome and does not look much like his mother. No doubt he looks like his father.'

"'That is very possible,' replied the innkeeper; 'but we never knew whose child it was. She died without telling any one, and no one here knew of her having a beau. Every one was hugely astonished when they heard she was enceinte, and no one would believe it.'

"A sort of unpleasant chill came over me, one of those painful surface wounds that affect us like the shadow of an impending sorrow. And I looked at the man in the yard. He had just drawn water for the horses and was carrying two buckets, limping as he walked, with a painful effort of his shorter leg. His clothes were ragged, he was hideously dirty, with long yellow hair, so tangled that it looked like strands of rope falling down at either side of his face.

"'He is not worth much,' continued the innkeeper; 'we have kept him for charity's sake. Perhaps he would have turned out better if he had been brought up like other folks. But what could one do, monsieur? No father, no mother, no money! My parents took pity on him, but he was not their child, you understand.'

"I said nothing.

"I slept in my old room, and all night long I thought of this frightful stableman, saying to myself: 'Supposing it is my own son? Could I have caused that girl's death and procreated this being? It was quite possible!'

"I resolved to speak to this man and to find out the exact date of his birth. A variation of two months would set my doubts at rest.

"I sent for him the next day. But he could not speak French. He looked as if he could not understand anything, being absolutely ignorant of his age, which I had inquired of him through one of the maids. He stood before me like an idiot, twirling his hat in 'his knotted, disgusting hands, laughing stupidly, with something of his mother's laugh in the corners of his mouth and of his eyes.

"The landlord, appearing on the scene, went to look for the birth certificate of this wretched being. He was born eight months and twenty-six days after my stay at Pont Labbe, for I recollect perfectly that we reached Lorient on the fifteenth of August. The certificate contained this description: 'Father unknown.' The mother called herself Jeanne Kerradec.

"Then my heart began to beat rapidly. I could not utter a word, for I felt as if I were choking. I looked at this animal whose long yellow hair reminded me of a straw heap, and the beggar, embarrassed by my gaze, stopped laughing, turned his head aside, and wanted to get away.

"All day long I wandered beside the little river, giving way to painful reflections. But what was the use of reflection? I could be sure of nothing. For hours and hours I weighed all the pros and cons in favor of or against the probability of my being the father, growing nervous over inexplicable suppositions, only to return incessantly to the same horrible uncertainty, then to the still more atrocious conviction that this man was my son.

"I could eat no dinner, and went to my room.

"I lay awake for a long time, and when I finally fell asleep I was haunted by horrible visions. I saw this laborer laughing in my face and calling me 'papa.' Then he changed into a dog and bit the calves of my legs, and no matter how fast I ran he still followed me, and instead of barking, talked and reviled me. Then he appeared before my colleagues at the Academy, who had assembled to decide whether I was really his father; and one of them cried out: 'There can be no doubt about it! See how he resembles him.' And, indeed, I could see that this monster looked like me. And I awoke with this idea fixed in my mind and with an insane desire to see the man again and assure myself whether or not we had similar features.

"I joined him as he was going to mass (it was Sunday) and I gave him five francs as I gazed at him anxiously. He began to laugh in an idiotic manner, took the money, and then, embarrassed afresh at my gaze, he ran off, after stammering an almost inarticulate word that, no doubt, meant 'thank you.'

"My day passed in the same distress of mind as on the previous night. I sent for the landlord, and, with the greatest caution, skill and tact, I told him that I was interested in this poor creature, so abandoned by every one and deprived of everything, and I wished to do something for him.

"But the man replied: 'Oh, do not think of it, monsieur; he is of no account; you will only cause yourself annoyance. I employ him to clean out the stable, and that is all he can do. I give him his board and let him sleep with the horses. He needs nothing more. If you have an old pair of trousers, you might give them to him, but they will be in rags in a week.'

"I did not insist, intending to think it over.

"The poor wretch came home that evening frightfully drunk, came near setting fire to the house, killed a horse by hitting it with a pickaxe, and ended up by lying down to sleep in the mud in the midst of the pouring rain, thanks to my donation.

"They begged me next day not to give him any more money. Brandy drove him crazy, and as soon as he had two sous in his pocket he would spend it in drink. The landlord added: 'Giving him money is like trying to kill him.' The man had never, never in his life had more than a few centimes, thrown to him by travellers, and he knew of no destination for this metal but the wine shop.

"I spent several hours in my room with an open book before me which I pretended to read, but in reality looking at this animal, my son! my son! trying to discover if he looked anything like me. After careful scrutiny I seemed to recognize a similarity in the lines of the forehead and the root of the nose, and I was soon convinced that there was a resemblance, concealed by the difference in garb and the man's hideous head of hair.

"I could not stay here any longer without arousing suspicion, and I went away, my heart crushed, leaving with the innkeeper some money to soften the existence of his servant.

"For six years now I have lived with this idea in my mind, this horrible uncertainty, this abominable suspicion. And each year an irresistible force takes me back to Pont Labbe. Every year I condemn myself to the torture of seeing this animal raking the manure, imagining that he resembles me, and endeavoring, always vainly, to render him some assistance. And each year I return more uncertain, more tormented, more worried.

"I tried to have him taught, but he is a hopeless idiot. I tried to make his life less hard. He is an irreclaimable drunkard, and spends in drink all the money one gives him, and knows enough to sell his new clothes in order to get brandy.

"I tried to awaken his master's sympathy, so that he should look after him, offering to pay him for doing so. The innkeeper, finally surprised, said, very wisely: 'All that you do for him, monsieur, will only help to destroy him. He must be kept like a prisoner. As soon as he has any spare time, or any comfort, he becomes wicked. If you wish to do good, there is no lack of abandoned children, but select one who will appreciate your attention.'

"What could I say?

"If I allowed the slightest suspicion of the doubts that tortured me to escape, this idiot would assuredly become cunning, in order to blackmail me, to compromise me and ruin me. He would call out 'papa,' as in my dream.

"And I said to myself that I had killed the mother and lost this atrophied creature, this larva of the stable, born and raised amid the manure, this man who, if brought up like others, would have been like others.

"And you cannot imagine what a strange, embarrassed and intolerable feeling comes over me when he stands before me and I reflect that he came from myself, that he belongs to me through the intimate bond that links father and son, that, thanks to the terrible law of heredity, he is my own self in a thousand ways, in his blood and his flesh, and that he has even the same germs of disease, the same leaven of emotions.

"I have an incessant restless, distressing longing to see him, and the sight of him causes me intense suffering, as I look down from my window and watch him for hours removing and carting the horse manure, saying to myself: 'That is my son.'

"And I sometimes feel an irresistible longing to embrace him. I have never even touched his dirty hand."

The academician was silent. His companion, a tactful man, murmured: "Yes, indeed, we ought to take a closer interest in children who have no father."

A gust of wind passing through the tree shook its yellow clusters, enveloping in a fragrant and delicate mist the two old men, who inhaled in the fragrance with deep breaths.

The senator added: "It is good to be twenty-five and even to have children like that."

THAT PIG OF A MORIN

I

"Here, my friend," I said to Labarbe, "you have just repeated those five words, that pig of a Morin. Why on earth do I never hear Morin's name mentioned without his being called a pig?"

Labarbe, who is a deputy, looked at me with his owl-like eyes and said: "Do you mean to say that you do not know Morin's story and you come from La Rochelle?" I was obliged to declare that I did not know Morin's story, so Labarbe rubbed his hands and began his recital.

"You knew Morin, did you not, and you remember his large linen-draper's shop on the Quai de la Rochelle?"

"Yes, perfectly."

"Well, then. You must know that in 1862 or '63 Morin went to spend a fortnight in Paris for pleasure; or for his pleasures, but under the pretext of renewing his stock, and you also know what a fortnight in Paris means to a country shopkeeper; it fires his blood. The theatre every evening, women's dresses rustling up against you and continual excitement; one goes almost mad with it. One sees nothing but dancers in tights, actresses in very low dresses, round legs, fat shoulders, all nearly within reach of one's hands, without daring, or being able, to touch them, and one scarcely tastes food. When one leaves the city one's heart is still all in a flutter and one's mind still exhilarated by a sort of longing for kisses which tickles one's lips.

"Morin was in that condition when he took his ticket for La Rochelle by the eight-forty night express. As he was walking up and down the waiting-room at the station he stopped suddenly in front of a young lady who was kissing an old one. She had her veil up, and Morin murmured with delight: 'By Jove what a pretty woman!'

"When she had said 'good-by' to the old lady she went into the waiting-room, and Morin followed her; then she went on the platform and Morin still followed her; then she got into an empty carriage, and he again followed her. There were very few travellers on the express. The engine whistled and the train started. They were alone. Morin devoured her with his eyes. She appeared to be about nineteen or twenty and was fair, tall, with a bold look. She wrapped a railway rug round her and stretched herself on the seat to sleep.

"Morin asked himself: 'I wonder who she is?' And a thousand conjectures, a thousand projects went through his head. He said to himself: 'So many adventures are told as happening on railway journeys that this may be one that is going to present itself to me. Who knows? A piece of good luck like that happens very suddenly, and perhaps I need only be a little venturesome. Was it not Danton who said: "Audacity, more audacity and always audacity"? If it was not Danton it was Mirabeau, but that does not matter. But then I have no audacity, and that is the difficulty. Oh! If one only knew, if one could only read people's minds! I will bet that every day one passes by magnificent opportunities without knowing it, though a gesture would be enough to let me know her mind.'

"Then he imagined to himself combinations which conducted him to triumph. He pictured some chivalrous deed or merely some slight service which he rendered her, a lively, gallant conversation which ended in a declaration.

"But he could find no opening, had no pretext, and he waited for some fortunate circumstance, with his heart beating and his mind topsy-turvy. The night passed and the pretty girl still slept, while Morin was meditating his own fall. The day broke and soon the first ray of sunlight appeared in the sky, a long, clear ray which shone on the face of the sleeping girl and woke her. She sat up, looked at the country, then at Morin and smiled. She smiled like a happy woman, with an engaging and bright look, and Morin trembled. Certainly that smile was intended for him; it was discreet invitation, the signal which he was waiting for. That smile meant to say: 'How stupid, what a ninny, what a dolt, what a donkey you are, to have sat there on your seat like a post all night!

"'Just look at me, am I not charming? And you have sat like that for the whole night, when you have been alone with a pretty woman, you great simpleton!'

"She was still smiling as she looked at him; she even began to laugh; and he lost his head trying to find something suitable to say, no matter what. But he could think of nothing, nothing, and then, seized with a coward's courage, he said to himself:

"'So much the worse, I will risk everything,' and suddenly, without the slightest warning, he went toward her, his arms extended, his lips protruding, and, seizing her in his arms, he kissed her.

"She sprang up immediately with a bound, crying out: 'Help! help!' and screaming with terror; and then she opened the carriage door and waved her arm out, mad with terror and trying to jump out, while Morin, who was almost distracted and feeling sure that she would throw herself out, held her by the skirt and stammered: 'Oh, madame! oh, madame!'

"The train slackened speed and then stopped. Two guards rushed up at the young woman's frantic signals. She threw herself into their arms, stammering: 'That man wanted—wanted—to—to—' And then she fainted.

"They were at Mauze station, and the gendarme on duty arrested Morin. When the victim of his indiscreet admiration had regained her consciousness, she made her charge against him, and the police drew it up. The poor linen draper did not reach home till night, with a prosecution hanging over him for an outrage to morals in a public place."

II

"At that time I was editor of the Fanal des Charentes, and I used to meet Morin every day at the Cafe du Commerce, and the day after his adventure. he came to see me, as he did not know what to do. I did not hide my opinion from him, but said to him: 'You are no better than a pig. No decent man behaves like that.'

"He cried. His wife had given him a beating, and he foresaw his trade ruined, his name dragged through the mire and dishonored, his friends scandalized and taking no notice of him. In the end he excited my pity, and I sent for my colleague, Rivet, a jocular but very sensible little man, to give us his advice.

"He advised me to see the public prosecutor, who was a friend of mine, and so I sent Morin home and went to call on the magistrate. He told me that the woman who had been insulted was a young lady, Mademoiselle Henriette Bonnel, who had just received her certificate as governess in Paris and spent her holidays with her uncle and aunt, who were very respectable tradespeople in Mauze. What made Morin's case all the more serious was that the uncle had lodged a complaint, but the public official had consented to let the matter drop if this complaint were withdrawn, so we must try and get him to do this.

"I went back to Morin's and found him in bed, ill with excitement and distress. His wife, a tall raw-boned woman with a beard, was abusing him continually, and she showed me into the room, shouting at me: 'So you have come to see that pig of a Morin. Well, there he is, the darling!' And she planted herself in front of the bed, with her hands on her hips. I told him how matters stood, and he begged me to go and see the girl's uncle and aunt. It was a delicate mission, but I undertook it, and the poor devil never ceased repeating: 'I assure you I did not even kiss her; no, not even that. I will take my oath to it!'

"I replied: 'It is all the same; you are nothing but a pig.' And I took a thousand francs which he gave me to employ as I thought best, but as I did not care to venture to her uncle's house alone, I begged Rivet to go with me, which he agreed to do on condition that we went immediately, for he had some urgent business at La Rochelle that afternoon. So two hours later we rang at the door of a pretty country house. An attractive girl came and opened the door to us assuredly the young lady in question, and I said to Rivet in a low voice: 'Confound it! I begin to understand Morin!'

"The uncle, Monsieur Tonnelet, subscribed to the Fanal, and was a fervent political coreligionist of ours. He received us with open arms and congratulated us and wished us joy; he was delighted at having the two editors in his house, and Rivet whispered to me: 'I think we shall be able to arrange the matter of that pig of a Morin for him.'

"The niece had left the room and I introduced the delicate subject. I waved the spectre of scandal before his eyes; I accentuated the inevitable depreciation which the young lady would suffer if such an affair became known, for nobody would believe in a simple kiss, and the good man seemed undecided, but he could not make up his mind about anything without his wife, who would not be in until late that evening. But suddenly he uttered an exclamation of triumph: 'Look here, I have an excellent idea; I will keep you here to dine and sleep, and when my wife comes home I hope we shall be able to arrange matters:

"Rivet resisted at first, but the wish to extricate that pig of a Morin decided him, and we accepted the invitation, and the uncle got up radiant, called his niece and proposed that we should take a stroll in his grounds, saying: 'We will leave serious matters until the morning.' Rivet and he began to talk politics, while I soon found myself lagging a little behind with 'the girl who was really charming—charming—and with the greatest precaution I began to speak to her about her adventure and try to make her my ally. She did not, however, appear the least confused, and listened to me like a person who was enjoying the whole thing very much.

"I said to her: 'Just think, mademoiselle, how unpleasant it will be for you. You will have to appear in court, to encounter malicious looks, to speak before everybody and to recount that unfortunate occurrence in the railway carriage in public. Do you not think, between ourselves, that it would have been much better for you to have put that dirty scoundrel back in his place without calling for assistance, and merely to change your carriage?' She began to laugh and replied: 'What you say is quite true, but what could I do? I was frightened, and when one is frightened one does not stop to reason with one's self. As soon as I realized the situation I was very sorry, that I had called out, but then it was too late. You must also remember that the idiot threw himself upon me like a madman, without saying a word and looking like a lunatic. I did not even know what he wanted of me.'

"She looked me full in the face without being nervous or intimidated and I said to myself: 'She is a queer sort of girl, that: I can quite see how that pig Morin came to make a mistake,' and I went on jokingly: 'Come, mademoiselle, confess that he was excusable, for, after all, a man cannot find himself opposite such a pretty girl as you are without feeling a natural desire to kiss her.'

"She laughed more than ever and showed her teeth and said: 'Between the desire and the act, monsieur, there is room for respect.' It was an odd expression to use, although it was not very clear, and I asked abruptly: 'Well, now, suppose I were to kiss you, what would you do?' She stopped to look at me from head to foot and then said calmly: 'Oh, you? That is quite another matter.'

"I knew perfectly well, by Jove, that it was not the same thing at all, as everybody in the neighborhood called me 'Handsome Labarbe'—I was thirty years old in those days—but I asked her: 'And why, pray?' She shrugged her shoulders and replied: 'Well! because you are not so stupid as he is.' And then she added, looking at me slyly: 'Nor so ugly, either: And before she could make a movement to avoid me I had implanted a hearty kiss on her cheek. She sprang aside, but it was too late, and then she said: 'Well, you are not very bashful, either! But don't do that sort of thing again.'

"I put on a humble look and said in a low voice: 'Oh, mademoiselle! as for me, if I long for one thing more than another it is to be summoned before a magistrate for the same reason as Morin.'

"'Why?' she asked. And, looking steadily at her, I replied: 'Because you are one of the most beautiful creatures living; because it would be an honor and a glory for me to have wished to offer you violence, and because people would have said, after seeing you: "Well, Labarbe has richly deserved what he has got, but he is a lucky fellow, all the same."'

"She began to laugh heartily again and said: 'How funny you are!' And she had not finished the word 'funny' before I had her in my arms and was kissing her ardently wherever I could find a place, on her forehead, on her eyes, on her lips occasionally, on her cheeks, all over her head, some part of which she was obliged to leave exposed, in spite of herself, to defend the others; but at last she managed to release herself, blushing and angry. 'You are very unmannerly, monsieur,' she said, 'and I am sorry I listened to you.'

"I took her hand in some confusion and stammered out: 'I beg your pardon. I beg your pardon, mademoiselle. I have offended you; I have acted like a brute! Do not be angry with me for what I have done. If you knew—' I vainly sought for some excuse, and in a few moments she said: 'There is nothing for me to know, monsieur.' But I had found something to say, and I cried: 'Mademoiselle, I love you!'

"She was really surprised and raised her eyes to look at me, and I went on: 'Yes, mademoiselle, and pray listen to me. I do not know Morin, and I do not care anything about him. It does not matter to me the least if he is committed for trial and locked up meanwhile. I saw you here last year, and I was so taken with you that the thought of you has never left me since, and it does not matter to me whether you believe me or not. I thought you adorable, and the remembrance of you took such a hold on me that I longed to see you again, and so I made use of that fool Morin as a pretext, and here I am. Circumstances have made me exceed the due limits of respect, and I can only beg you to pardon me.'

"She looked at me to see if I was in earnest and was ready to smile again. Then she murmured: 'You humbug!' But I raised my hand and said in a sincere voice (and I really believe that I was sincere): 'I swear to you that I am speaking the truth,' and she replied quite simply: 'Don't talk nonsense!'

"We were alone, quite alone, as Rivet and her uncle had disappeared down a sidewalk, and I made her a real declaration of love, while I squeezed and kissed her hands, and she listened to it as to something new and agreeable, without exactly knowing how much of it she was to believe, while in the end I felt agitated, and at last really myself believed what I said. I was pale, anxious and trembling, and I gently put my arm round her waist and spoke to her softly, whispering into the little curls over her ears.

She seemed in a trance, so absorbed in thought was she.

"Then her hand touched mine, and she pressed it, and I gently squeezed her waist with a trembling, and gradually firmer, grasp. She did not move now, and I touched her cheek with my lips, and suddenly without seeking them my lips met hers. It was a long, long kiss, and it would have lasted longer still if I had not heard a hm! hm! just behind me, at which she made her escape through the bushes, and turning round I saw Rivet coming toward me, and, standing in the middle of the path, he said without even smiling: 'So that is the way you settle the affair of that pig of a Morin.' And I replied conceitedly: 'One does what one can, my dear fellow. But what about the uncle? How have you got on with him? I will answer for the niece.' 'I have not been so fortunate with him,' he replied.

"Whereupon I took his arm and we went indoors."

III

"Dinner made me lose my head altogether. I sat beside her, and my hand continually met hers under the tablecloth, my foot touched hers and our glances met.

"After dinner we took a walk by moonlight, and I whispered all the tender things I could think of to her. I held her close to me, kissed her every moment, while her uncle and Rivet were arguing as they walked in front of us. They went in, and soon a messenger brought a telegram from her aunt, saying that she would not return until the next morning at seven o'clock by the first train.

"'Very well, Henriette,' her uncle said, 'go and show the gentlemen their rooms.' She showed Rivet his first, and he whispered to me: 'There was no danger of her taking us into yours first.' Then she took me to my room, and as soon as she was alone with me I took her in my arms again and tried to arouse her emotion, but when she saw the danger she escaped out of the room, and I retired very much put out and excited and feeling rather foolish, for I knew that I should not sleep much, and I was wondering how I could have committed such a mistake, when there was a gentle knock at my door, and on my asking who was there a low voice replied: 'I'

"I dressed myself quickly and opened the door, and she came in. 'I forgot to ask you what you take in the morning,' she said; 'chocolate, tea or coffee?' I put my arms round her impetuously and said, devouring her with kisses: 'I will take—I will take—'

"But she freed herself from my arms, blew out my candle and disappeared and left me alone in the dark, furious, trying to find some matches, and not able to do so. At last I got some and I went into the passage, feeling half mad, with my candlestick in my hand.

"What was I about to do? I did not stop to reason, I only wanted to find her, and I would. I went a few steps without reflecting, but then I suddenly thought: 'Suppose I should walk into the uncle's room what should I say?' And I stood still, with my head a void and my heart beating. But in a few moments I thought of an answer: 'Of course, I shall say that I was looking for Rivet's room to speak to him about an important matter,' and I began to inspect all the doors, trying to find hers, and at last I took hold of a handle at a venture, turned it and went in. There was Henriette, sitting on her bed and looking at me in tears. So I gently turned the key, and going up to her on tiptoe I said: 'I forgot to ask you for something to read, mademoiselle.'

"I was stealthily returning to my room when a rough hand seized me and a voice—it was Rivet's—whispered in my ear: 'So you have not yet quite settled that affair of Morin's?'

"At seven o'clock the next morning Henriette herself brought me a cup of chocolate. I never have drunk anything like it, soft, velvety, perfumed, delicious. I could hardly take away my lips from the cup, and she had hardly left the room when Rivet came in. He seemed nervous and irritable, like a man who had not slept, and he said to me crossly:

"'If you go on like this you will end by spoiling the affair of that pig of a Morin!'

"At eight o'clock the aunt arrived. Our discussion was very short, for they withdrew their complaint, and I left five hundred francs for the poor of the town. They wanted to keep us for the day, and they arranged an excursion to go and see some ruins. Henriette made signs to me to stay, behind her parents' back, and I accepted, but Rivet was determined to go, and though I took him aside and begged and prayed him to do this for me, he appeared quite exasperated and kept saying to me: 'I have had enough of that pig of a Morin's affair, do you hear?'

"Of course I was obliged to leave also, and it was one of the hardest moments of my life. I could have gone on arranging that business as long as I lived, and when we were in the railway carriage, after shaking hands with her in silence, I said to Rivet: 'You are a mere brute!' And he replied: 'My dear fellow, you were beginning to annoy me confoundedly.'

"On getting to the Fanal office, I saw a crowd waiting for us, and as soon as they saw us they all exclaimed: 'Well, have you settled the affair of that pig of a Morin?' All La Rochelle was excited about it, and Rivet, who had got over his ill-humor on the journey, had great difficulty in keeping himself from laughing as he said: 'Yes, we have managed it, thanks to Labarbe: And we went to Morin's.

"He was sitting in an easy-chair with mustard plasters on his legs and cold bandages on his head, nearly dead with misery. He was coughing with the short cough of a dying man, without any one knowing how he had caught it, and his wife looked at him like a tigress ready to eat him, and as soon as he saw us he trembled so violently as to make his hands and knees shake, so I said to him immediately: 'It is all settled, you dirty scamp, but don't do such a thing again.'

"He got up, choking, took my hands and kissed them as if they had belonged to a prince, cried, nearly fainted, embraced Rivet and even kissed Madame Morin, who gave him such a push as to send him staggering back into his chair; but he never got over the blow; his mind had been too much upset. In all the country round, moreover, he was called nothing but 'that pig of a Morin,' and that epithet went through him like a sword-thrust every time he heard it. When a street boy called after him 'Pig!' he turned his head instinctively. His friends also overwhelmed him with horrible jokes and used to ask him, whenever they were eating ham, 'Is it a bit of yourself?' He died two years later.

"As for myself, when I was a candidate for the Chamber of Deputies in 1875, I called on the new notary at Fousserre, Monsieur Belloncle, to solicit his vote, and a tall, handsome and evidently wealthy lady received me. 'You do not know me again?' she said. And I stammered out: 'Why—no—madame.' 'Henriette Bonnel.' 'Ah!' And I felt myself turning pale, while she seemed perfectly at her ease and looked at me with a smile.

"As soon as she had left me alone with her husband he took both my hands, and, squeezing them as if he meant to crush them, he said: 'I have been intending to go and see you for a long time, my dear sir, for my wife has very often talked to me about you. I know—yes, I know under what painful circumstances you made her acquaintance, and I know also how perfectly you behaved, how full of delicacy, tact and devotion you showed yourself in the affair—' He hesitated and then said in a lower tone, as if he had been saying something low and coarse, 'in the affair of that pig of a Morin.'"

SAINT ANTHONY

They called him Saint Anthony, because his name was Anthony, and also, perhaps, because he was a good fellow, jovial, a lover of practical jokes, a tremendous eater and a heavy drinker and a gay fellow, although he was sixty years old.

He was a big peasant of the district of Caux, with a red face, large chest and stomach, and perched on two legs that seemed too slight for the bulk of his body.

He was a widower and lived alone with his two men servants and a maid on his farm, which he conducted with shrewd economy. He was careful of his own interests, understood business and the raising of cattle, and farming. His two sons and his three daughters, who had married well, were living in the neighborhood and came to dine with their father once a month. His vigor of body was famous in all the countryside. "He is as strong as Saint Anthony," had become a kind of proverb.

At the time of the Prussian invasion Saint Anthony, at the wine shop, promised to eat an army, for he was a braggart, like a true Norman, a bit of a coward and a blusterer. He banged his fist on the wooden table, making the cups and the brandy glasses dance, and cried with the assumed wrath of a good fellow, with a flushed face and a sly look in his eye: "I shall have to eat some of them, nom de Dieu!" He reckoned that the Prussians would not come as far as Tanneville, but when he heard they were at Rautot he never went out of the house, and constantly watched the road from the little window of his kitchen, expecting at any moment to see the bayonets go by.

One morning as he was eating his luncheon with the servants the door opened and the mayor of the commune, Maitre Chicot, appeared, followed by a soldier wearing a black copper-pointed helmet. Saint Anthony bounded to his feet and his servants all looked at him, expecting to see him slash the Prussian. But he merely shook hands with the mayor, who said:

"Here is one for you, Saint Anthony. They came last night. Don't do anything foolish, above all things, for they talked of shooting and burning everything if there is the slightest unpleasantness, I have given you warning. Give him something to eat; he looks like a good fellow. Good-day. I am going to call on the rest. There are enough for all." And he went out.

Father Anthony, who had turned pale, looked at the Prussian. He was a big, young fellow with plump, white skin, blue eyes, fair hair, unshaven to his cheek bones, who looked stupid, timid and good. The shrewd Norman read him at once, and, reassured, he made him a sign to sit down. Then he said: "Will you take some soup?"

The stranger did not understand. Anthony then became bolder, and pushing a plateful of soup right under his nose, he said: "Here, swallow that, big pig!"

The soldier answered "Ya," and began to eat greedily, while the farmer, triumphant, feeling he had regained his reputation, winked his eye at the servants, who were making strange grimaces, what with their terror and their desire to laugh.

When the Prussian had devoured his soup, Saint Anthony gave him another plateful, which disappeared in like manner; but he flinched at the third which the farmer tried to insist on his eating, saying: "Come, put that into your stomach; 'twill fatten you or it is your own fault, eh, pig!"

The soldier, understanding only that they wanted to make him eat all his soup, laughed in a contented manner, making a sign to show that he could not hold any more.

Then Saint Anthony, become quite familiar, tapped him on the stomach, saying: "My, there is plenty in my pig's belly!" But suddenly he began to writhe with laughter, unable to speak. An idea had struck him which made him choke with mirth. "That's it, that's it, Saint Anthony and his pig. There's my pig!" And the three servants burst out laughing in their turn.

The old fellow was so pleased that he had the brandy brought in, good stuff, 'fil en dix', and treated every one. They clinked glasses with the Prussian, who clacked his tongue by way of flattery to show that he enjoyed it. And Saint Anthony exclaimed in his face: "Eh, is not that superfine? You don't get anything like that in your home, pig!"

From that time Father Anthony never went out without his Prussian. He had got what he wanted. This was his vengeance, the vengeance of an old rogue. And the whole countryside, which was in terror, laughed to split its sides at Saint Anthony's joke. Truly, there was no one like him when it came to humor. No one but he would have thought of a thing like that. He was a born joker!

He went to see his neighbors every day, arm in arm with his German, whom he introduced in a jovial manner, tapping him on the shoulder: "See, here is my pig; look and see if he is not growing fat, the animal!"

And the peasants would beam with smiles. "He is so comical, that reckless fellow, Antoine!"

"I will sell him to you, Cesaire, for three pistoles" (thirty francs).

"I will take him, Antoine, and I invite you to eat some black pudding."

"What I want is his feet."

"Feel his belly; you will see that it is all fat."

And they all winked at each other, but dared not laugh too loud, for fear the Prussian might finally suspect they were laughing at him. Anthony, alone growing bolder every day, pinched his thighs, exclaiming, "Nothing but fat"; tapped him on the back, shouting, "That is all bacon"; lifted him up in his arms as an old Colossus that could have lifted an anvil, declaring, "He weighs six hundred and no waste."

He had got into the habit of making people offer his "pig" something to eat wherever they went together. This was the chief pleasure, the great diversion every day. "Give him whatever you please, he will swallow everything." And they offered the man bread and butter, potatoes, cold meat, chitterlings, which caused the remark, "Some of your own, and choice ones."

The soldier, stupid and gentle, ate from politeness, charmed at these attentions, making himself ill rather than refuse, and he was actually growing fat and his uniform becoming tight for him. This delighted Saint Anthony, who said: "You know, my pig, that we shall have to have another cage made for you."

They had, however, become the best friends in the world, and when the old fellow went to attend to his business in the neighborhood the Prussian accompanied him for the simple pleasure of being with him.

The weather was severe; it was freezing hard. The terrible winter of 1870 seemed to bring all the scourges on France at one time.

Father Antoine, who made provision beforehand, and took advantage of every opportunity, foreseeing that manure would be scarce for the spring farming, bought from a neighbor who happened to be in need of money all that he had, and it was agreed that he should go every evening with his cart to get a load.

So every day at twilight he set out for the farm of Haules, half a league distant, always accompanied by his "pig." And each time it was a festival, feeding the animal. All the neighbors ran over there as they would go to high mass on Sunday.

But the soldier began to suspect something, be mistrustful, and when they laughed too loud he would roll his eyes uneasily, and sometimes they lighted up with anger.

One evening when he had eaten his fill he refused to swallow another morsel, and attempted to rise to leave the table. But Saint Anthony stopped him by a turn of the wrist and, placing his two powerful hands on his shoulders, he sat him down again so roughly that the chair smashed under him.

A wild burst of laughter broke forth, and Anthony, beaming, picked up his pig, acted as though he were dressing his wounds, and exclaimed: "Since you will not eat, you shall drink, nom de Dieu!" And they went to the wine shop to get some brandy.

The soldier rolled his eyes, which had a wicked expression, but he drank, nevertheless; he drank as long as they wanted him, and Saint Anthony held his head to the great delight of his companions.

The Norman, red as a tomato, his eyes ablaze, filled up the glasses and clinked, saying: "Here's to you!". And the Prussian, without speaking a word, poured down one after another glassfuls of cognac.

It was a contest, a battle, a revenge! Who would drink the most, nom d'un nom! They could neither of them stand any more when the liter was emptied. But neither was conquered. They were tied, that was all. They would have to begin again the next day.

They went out staggering and started for home, walking beside the dung cart which was drawn along slowly by two horses.

Snow began to fall and the moonless night was sadly lighted by this dead whiteness on the plain. The men began to feel the cold, and this aggravated their intoxication. Saint Anthony, annoyed at not being the victor, amused himself by shoving his companion so as to make him fall over into the ditch. The other would dodge backwards, and each time he did he uttered some German expression in an angry tone, which made the peasant roar with laughter. Finally the Prussian lost his temper, and just as Anthony was rolling towards him he responded with such a terrific blow with his fist that the Colossus staggered.

Then, excited by the brandy, the old man seized the pugilist round the waist, shook him for a few moments as he would have done with a little child, and pitched him at random to the other side of the road. Then, satisfied with this piece of work, he crossed his arms and began to laugh afresh.

But the soldier picked himself up in a hurry, his head bare, his helmet having rolled off, and drawing his sword he rushed over to Father Anthony.

When he saw him coming the peasant seized his whip by the top of the handle, his big holly wood whip, straight, strong and supple as the sinew of an ox.

The Prussian approached, his head down, making a lunge with his sword, sure of killing his adversary. But the old fellow, squarely hitting the blade, the point of which would have pierced his stomach, turned it aside, and with the butt end of the whip struck the soldier a sharp blow on the temple and he fell to the ground.

Then he, gazed aghast, stupefied with amazement, at the body, twitching convulsively at first and then lying prone and motionless. He bent over it, turned it on its back, and gazed at it for some time. The man's eyes were closed, and blood trickled from a wound at the side of his forehead. Although it was dark, Father Anthony could distinguish the bloodstain on the white snow.

He remained there, at his wit's end, while his cart continued slowly on its way.

What was he to do? He would be shot! They would burn his farm, ruin his district! What should he do? What should he do? How could he hide the body, conceal the fact of his death, deceive the Prussians? He heard voices in the distance, amid the utter stillness of the snow. All at once he roused himself, and picking up the helmet he placed it on his victim's head. Then, seizing him round the body, he lifted him up in his arms, and thus running with him, he overtook his team, and threw the body on top of the manure. Once in his own house he would think up some plan.

He walked slowly, racking his brain, but without result. He saw, he felt, that he was lost. He entered his courtyard. A light was shining in one of the attic windows; his maid was not asleep. He hastily backed his wagon to the edge of the manure hollow. He thought that by overturning the manure the body lying on top of it would fall into the ditch and be buried beneath it, and he dumped the cart.

As he had foreseen, the man was buried beneath the manure. Anthony evened it down with his fork, which he stuck in the ground beside it. He called his stableman, told him to put up the horses, and went to his room.

He went to bed, still thinking of what he had best do, but no ideas came to him. His apprehension increased in the quiet of his room. They would shoot him! He was bathed in perspiration from fear, his teeth chattered, he rose shivering, not being able to stay in bed.

He went downstairs to the kitchen, took the bottle of brandy from the sideboard and carried it upstairs. He drank two large glasses, one after another, adding a fresh intoxication to the late one, without quieting his mental anguish. He had done a pretty stroke of work, nom de Dieu, idiot!

He paced up and down, trying to think of some stratagem, some explanations, some cunning trick, and from time to time he rinsed his mouth with a swallow of "fil en dix" to give him courage.

But no ideas came to him, not one.

Towards midnight his watch dog, a kind of cross wolf called "Devorant," began to howl frantically. Father Anthony shuddered to the marrow of his bones, and each time the beast began his long and lugubrious wail the old man's skin turned to goose flesh.

He had sunk into a chair, his legs weak, stupefied, done up, waiting anxiously for "Devorant" to set up another howl, and starting convulsively from nervousness caused by terror.

The clock downstairs struck five. The dog was still howling. The peasant was almost insane. He rose to go and let the dog loose, so that he should not hear him. He went downstairs, opened the hall door, and stepped out into the darkness. The snow was still falling. The earth was all white, the farm buildings standing out like black patches. He approached the kennel. The dog was dragging at his chain. He unfastened it. "Devorant" gave a bound, then stopped short, his hair bristling, his legs rigid, his muzzle in the air, his nose pointed towards the manure heap.

Saint Anthony, trembling from head to foot, faltered:

"What's the matter with you, you dirty hound?" and he walked a few steps forward, gazing at the indistinct outlines, the sombre shadow of the courtyard.

Then he saw a form, the form of a man sitting on the manure heap!

He gazed at it, paralyzed by fear, and breathing hard. But all at once he saw, close by, the handle of the manure fork which was sticking in the ground. He snatched it up and in one of those transports of fear that will make the greatest coward brave he rushed forward to see what it was.

It was he, his Prussian, come to life, covered with filth from his bed of manure which had kept him warm. He had sat down mechanically, and remained there in the snow which sprinkled down, all covered with dirt and blood as he was, and still stupid from drinking, dazed by the blow and exhausted from his wound.

He perceived Anthony, and too sodden to understand anything, he made an attempt to rise. But the moment the old man recognized him, he foamed with rage like a wild animal.

"Ah, pig! pig!" he sputtered. "You are not dead! You are going to denounce me now—wait—wait!"

And rushing on the German with all the strength of leis arms he flung the raised fork like a lance and buried the four prongs full length in his breast.

The soldier fell over on his back, uttering a long death moan, while the old peasant, drawing the fork out of his breast, plunged it over and over again into his abdomen, his stomach, his throat, like a madman, piercing the body from head to foot, as it still quivered, and the blood gushed out in streams.

Finally he stopped, exhausted by his arduous work, swallowing great mouthfuls of air, calmed down at the completion of the murder.

As the cocks were beginning to crow in the poultry yard and it was near daybreak, he set to work to bury the man.

He dug a hole in the manure till he reached the earth, dug down further, working wildly, in a frenzy of strength with frantic motions of his arms and body.

When the pit was deep enough he rolled the corpse into it with the fork, covered it with earth, which he stamped down for some time, and then put back the manure, and he smiled as he saw the thick snow finishing his work and covering up its traces with a white sheet.

He then stuck the fork in the manure and went into the house. His bottle, still half full of brandy stood on the table. He emptied it at a draught, threw himself on his bed and slept heavily.

He woke up sober, his mind calm and clear, capable of judgment and thought.

At the end of an hour he was going about the country making inquiries everywhere for his soldier. He went to see the Prussian officer to find out why they had taken away his man.

As everyone knew what good friends they were, no one suspected him. He even directed the research, declaring that the Prussian went to see the girls every evening.

An old retired gendarme who had an inn in the next village, and a pretty daughter, was arrested and shot.

LASTING LOVE

*I*t was the end of the dinner that opened the shooting season. The Marquis de Bertrans with his guests sat around a brightly lighted table, covered with fruit and flowers. The conversation drifted to love. Immediately there arose an animated discussion, the same eternal discussion as to whether it were possible to love more than once. Examples were given of persons who had loved once; these were offset by those who had loved violently many times. The men agreed that passion, like sickness, may attack the same person several times, unless it strikes to kill. This conclusion seemed quite incontestable. The women, however, who based their opinion on poetry rather than on practical observation, maintained that love, the great passion, may come only once to mortals. It resembles lightning, they said, this love. A heart once touched by it becomes forever such a waste, so ruined, so consumed, that no other strong sentiment can take root there, not even a dream. The marquis, who had indulged in many love affairs, disputed this belief.

"I tell you it is possible to love several times with all one's heart and soul. You quote examples of persons who have killed themselves for love, to prove the impossibility of a second passion. I wager that if they had not foolishly committed suicide, and so destroyed the possibility of a second experience, they would have found a new love, and still another, and so on till death. It is with love as with drink. He who has once indulged is forever a slave. It is a thing of temperament."

They chose the old doctor as umpire. He thought it was as the marquis had said, a thing of temperament.

"As for me," he said, "I once knew of a love which lasted fifty-five years without one day's respite, and which ended only with death." The wife of the marquis clasped her hands.

"That is beautiful! Ah, what a dream to be loved in such a way! What bliss to live for fifty-five years enveloped in an intense, unwavering affection! How this happy being must have blessed his life to be so adored!"

The doctor smiled.

"You are not mistaken, madame, on this point the loved one was a man. You even know him; it is Monsieur Chouquet, the chemist. As to the woman, you also know her, the old chair-mender, who came every year to the chateau." The enthusiasm of the women fell. Some expressed their contempt with "Pouah!" for the loves of common people did not interest them. The doctor continued: "Three months ago I was called to the deathbed of the old chair-mender. The priest had preceded me. She wished to make us the executors of her will. In order that we might understand her conduct, she told us the story of her life. It is most singular and touching: Her father and mother were both chair-menders. She had never lived in a house. As a little child she wandered about with them, dirty, unkempt, hungry. They visited many towns, leaving their horse, wagon and dog just outside the limits, where the child played in the grass alone until her parents had repaired all the broken chairs in the place. They seldom spoke, except to cry, 'Chairs! Chairs! Chair-mender!'

"When the little one strayed too far away, she would be called back by the harsh, angry voice of her father. She never heard a word of affection. When she grew older, she fetched and carried the broken chairs. Then it was she made friends with the children in the street, but their parents always called them away and scolded them for speaking to the barefooted child. Often the boys threw stones at her. Once a kind woman gave her a few pennies. She saved them most carefully.

"One day—she was then eleven years old—as she was walking through a country town she met, behind the cemetery, little Chouquet, weeping bitterly, because one of his playmates had stolen two precious liards (mills). The tears of the small bourgeois, one of those much-envied mortals, who, she imagined, never knew trouble, completely upset her. She approached him and, as soon as she learned the cause of his grief, she put into his hands all her savings. He took them without hesitation and dried his eyes. Wild with joy, she kissed him. He was busy counting his money, and did not object. Seeing that she was not repulsed, she threw her arms round him and gave him a hug—then she ran away.

"What was going on in her poor little head? Was it because she had sacrificed all her fortune that she became madly fond of this youngster, or was it because she had given him the first tender kiss? The mystery is alike for children and for those of riper years. For months she dreamed of that corner near the cemetery and of the little chap. She stole a sou here and, there from her parents on the chair money or groceries she was sent to buy. When she returned to the spot near the cemetery she had two francs in her pocket, but he was not there. Passing his father's drug store, she caught sight of him behind the counter. He was sitting between a large red globe and a blue one. She only loved him the more, quite carried away at the sight of the brilliant-colored globes. She cherished the recollection of it forever in her heart. The following year she met him near the school playing marbles. She rushed up to him, threw her arms round him, and kissed him so passionately that he screamed, in fear. To quiet him, she gave him all her money. Three francs and twenty centimes! A real gold mine, at which he gazed with staring eyes.

"After this he allowed her to kiss him as much as she wished. During the next four years she put into his hands all her savings, which he pocketed conscientiously in exchange for kisses. At one time it was thirty sous, at another two francs. Again, she only had twelve sous. She wept with grief and shame, explaining brokenly that it had been a poor year. The next time she brought five francs, in one whole piece, which made her laugh with joy. She no longer thought of any one but the boy, and he watched for her with impatience; sometimes he would run to meet her. This made her heart thump with joy. Suddenly he disappeared. He had gone to boarding school. She found this out by careful investigation. Then she used great diplomacy to persuade her parents to change their route and pass by this way again during vacation. After a year of scheming she succeeded. She had not seen him for two years, and scarcely recognized him, he was so changed, had grown taller, better looking and was imposing in his uniform, with its brass buttons. He pretended not to see her, and passed by without a glance. She wept for two days and from that time loved and suffered unceasingly.

"Every year he came home and she passed him, not daring to lift her eyes. He never condescended to turn his head toward her. She loved him madly, hopelessly. She said to me:

"'He is the only man whom I have ever seen. I don't even know if another exists.' Her parents died. She continued their work.

"One day, on entering the village, where her heart always remained, she saw Chouquet coming out of his pharmacy with a young lady leaning on his arm. She was his wife. That night the chair-mender threw herself into the river. A drunkard passing the spot pulled her out and took her to the drug store. Young Chouquet came down in his dressing gown to revive her. Without seeming to know who she was he undressed her and rubbed her;

then he said to her, in a harsh voice:

"'You are mad! People must not do stupid things like that.' His voice brought her to life again. He had spoken to her! She was happy for a long time. He refused remuneration for his trouble, although she insisted.

"All her life passed in this way. She worked, thinking always of him. She began to buy medicines at his pharmacy; this gave her a chance to talk to him and to see him closely. In this way, she was still able to give him money.

"As I said before, she died this spring. When she had closed her pathetic story she entreated me to take her earnings to the man she loved. She had worked only that she might leave him something to remind him of her after her death. I gave the priest fifty francs for her funeral expenses. The next morning I went to see the Chouquets. They were finishing breakfast, sitting opposite each other, fat and red, important and self-satisfied. They welcomed me and offered me some coffee, which I accepted. Then I began my story in a trembling voice, sure that they would be softened, even to tears. As soon as Chouquet understood that he had been loved by 'that vagabond! that chair-mender! that wanderer!' he swore with indignation as though his reputation had been sullied, the respect of decent people lost, his personal honor, something precious and dearer to him than life, gone. His exasperated wife kept repeating: 'That beggar! That beggar!'

"Seeming unable to find words suitable to the enormity, he stood up and began striding about. He muttered: 'Can you understand anything so horrible, doctor? Oh, if I had only known it while she was alive, I should have had her thrown into prison. I promise you she would not have escaped.'

"I was dumfounded; I hardly knew what to think or say, but I had to finish my mission. 'She commissioned me,' I said, 'to give you her savings, which amount to three thousand five hundred francs. As what I have just told you seems to be very disagreeable, perhaps you would prefer to give this money to the poor.'

"They looked at me, that man and woman,' speechless with amazement. I took the few thousand francs from out of my pocket. Wretched-looking money from every country. Pennies and gold pieces all mixed together. Then I asked:

"'What is your decision?'

"Madame Chouquet spoke first. 'Well, since it is the dying woman's wish, it seems to me impossible to refuse it.'

"Her husband said, in a shamefaced manner: 'We could buy something for our children with it.'

"I answered dryly: 'As you wish.'

"He replied: 'Well, give it to us anyhow, since she commissioned you to do so; we will find a way to put it to some good purpose.'

"I gave them the money, bowed and left.

"The next day Chouquet came to me and said brusquely:

"'That woman left her wagon here—what have you done with it?'

"'Nothing; take it if you wish.'

"'It's just what I wanted,' he added, and walked off. I called him back and said:

"'She also left her old horse and two dogs. Don't you need them?'

"He stared at me surprised: 'Well, no! Really, what would I do with them?'

"'Dispose of them as you like.'

"He laughed and held out his hand to me. I shook it. What could I do? The doctor and the druggist in a country village must not be at enmity. I have kept the dogs. The priest took the old horse. The wagon is useful to Chouquet, and with the money he has bought railroad stock. That is the only deep, sincere love that I have ever known in all my life."

The doctor looked up. The marquise, whose eyes were full of tears, sighed and said:

"There is no denying the fact, only women know how to love."

PIERROT

Mme. Lefevre was a country dame, a widow, one of these half peasants, with ribbons and bonnets with trimming on them, one of those persons who clipped her words and put on great airs in public, concealing the soul of a pretentious animal beneath a comical and bedizened exterior, just as the country-folks hide their coarse red hands in ecru silk gloves.

She had a servant, a good simple peasant, called Rose.

The two women lived in a little house with green shutters by the side of the high road in Normandy, in the centre of the country of Caux. As they had a narrow strip of garden in front of the house, they grew some vegetables.

One night someone stole twelve onions. As soon as Rose became aware of the theft, she ran to tell madame, who came downstairs in her woolen petticoat. It was a shame and a disgrace! They had robbed her, Mme. Lefevre! As there were thieves in the country, they might come back.

And the two frightened women examined the foot tracks, talking, and supposing all sorts of things.

"See, they went that way! They stepped on the wall, they jumped into the garden!"

And they became apprehensive for the future. How could they sleep in peace now!

The news of the theft spread. The neighbors came, making examinations and discussing the matter in their turn, while the two women explained to each newcomer what they had observed and their opinion.

A farmer who lived near said to them:

"You ought to have a dog."

That is true, they ought to have a dog, if it were only to give the alarm. Not a big dog. Heavens! what would they do with a big dog? He would eat their heads off. But a little dog (in Normandy they say "quin"), a little puppy who would bark.

As soon as everyone had left, Mme. Lefevre discussed this idea of a dog for some time. On reflection she made a thousand objections, terrified at the idea of a bowl full of soup, for she belonged to that race of parsimonious country women who always carry centimes in their pocket to give alms in public to beggars on the road and to put in the Sunday collection plate.

Rose, who loved animals, gave her opinion and defended it shrewdly. So it was decided that they should have a dog, a very small dog.

They began to look for one, but could find nothing but big dogs, who would devour enough soup to make one shudder. The grocer of Rolleville had one, a tiny one, but he demanded two francs to cover the cost of sending it. Mme. Lefevre declared that she would feed a "quin," but would not buy one.

The baker, who knew all that occurred, brought in his wagon one morning a strange little yellow animal, almost without paws, with the body of a crocodile, the head of a fox, and a curly tail—a true cockade, as big as all the rest of him. Mme. Lefevre thought this common cur that cost nothing was very handsome. Rose hugged it and asked what its name was.

"Pierrot," replied the baker.

The dog was installed in an old soap box and they gave it some water which it drank. They then offered it a piece of bread. He ate it. Mme. Lefevre, uneasy, had an idea.

"When he is thoroughly accustomed to the house we can let him run. He can find something to eat, roaming about the country."

They let him run, in fact, which did not prevent him from being famished. Also he never barked except to beg for food, and then he barked furiously.

Anyone might come into the garden, and Pierrot would run up and fawn on each one in turn and not utter a bark.

Mme. Lefevre, however, had become accustomed to the animal. She even went so far as to like it and to give it from time to time pieces of bread soaked in the gravy on her plate.

But she had not once thought of the dog tax, and when they came to collect eight francs—eight francs, madame—for this puppy who never even barked, she almost fainted from the shock.

It was immediately decided that they must get rid of Pierrot. No one wanted him. Every one declined to take him for ten leagues around. Then they resolved, not knowing what else to do, to make him "piquer du mas."

"Piquer du mas" means to eat chalk. When one wants to get rid of a dog they make him "Piquer du mas."

In the midst of an immense plain one sees a kind of hut, or rather a very small roof standing above the ground. This is the entrance to the clay pit. A big perpendicular hole is sunk for twenty metres underground and ends in a series of long subterranean tunnels.

Once a year they go down into the quarry at the time they fertilize the ground. The rest of the year it serves as a cemetery for condemned dogs, and as one passed by this hole plaintive howls, furious or despairing barks and lamentable appeals reach one's ear.

Sportsmen's dogs and sheep dogs flee in terror from this mournful place, and when one leans over it one perceives a disgusting odor of putrefaction.

Frightful dramas are enacted in the darkness.

When an animal has suffered down there for ten or twelve days, nourished on the foul remains of his predecessors, another animal, larger and more vigorous, is thrown into the hole. There they are, alone, starving, with glittering eyes. They watch each other, follow each other, hesitate in doubt. But hunger impels them; they attack each other, fight desperately for some time, and the stronger eats the weaker, devours him alive.

When it was decided to make Pierrot "piquer du mas" they looked round for an executioner. The laborer who mended the road demanded six sous to take the dog there. That seemed wildly exorbitant to Mme. Lefevre. The neighbor's hired boy wanted five sous; that was still too much. So Rose having observed that they had better carry it there themselves, as in that way it would not be brutally treated on the way and made to suspect its fate, they resolved to go together at twilight.

They offered the dog that evening a good dish of soup with a piece of butter in it. He swallowed every morsel of it, and as he wagged his tail with delight Rose put him in her apron.

They walked quickly, like thieves, across the plain. They soon perceived the chalk pit and walked up to it. Mme. Lefevre leaned over to hear if any animal was moaning. No, there were none there; Pierrot would be alone. Then Rose, who was crying, kissed the dog and threw him into the chalk pit, and they both leaned over, listening.

First they heard a dull sound, then the sharp, bitter, distracting cry of an animal in pain, then a succession of little mournful cries, then despairing appeals, the cries of a dog who is entreating, his head raised toward the opening of the pit.

He yelped, oh, how he yelped!

They were filled with remorse, with terror, with a wild inexplicable fear, and ran away from the spot. As Rose went faster Mme. Lefevre cried: "Wait for me, Rose, wait for me!"

At night they were haunted by frightful nightmares.

Mme. Lefevre dreamed she was sitting down at table to eat her soup, but when she uncovered the tureen Pierrot was in it. He jumped out and bit her nose.

She awoke and thought she heard him yelping still. She listened, but she was mistaken.

She fell asleep again and found herself on a high road, an endless road, which she followed. Suddenly in the middle of the road she perceived a basket, a large farmer's basket, lying there, and this basket frightened her.

She ended by opening it, and Pierrot, concealed in it, seized her hand and would not let go. She ran away in terror with the dog hanging to the end of her arm, which he held between his teeth.

At daybreak she arose, almost beside herself, and ran to the chalk pit.

He was yelping, yelping still; he had yelped all night. She began to sob and called him by all sorts of endearing names. He answered her with all the tender inflections of his dog's voice.

Then she wanted to see him again, promising herself that she would give him a good home till he died.

She ran to the chalk digger, whose business it was to excavate for chalk, and told him the situation. The man listened, but said nothing. When she had finished he said:

"You want your dog? That will cost four francs." She gave a jump. All her grief was at an end at once.

"Four francs!" she said. "You would die of it! Four francs!"

"Do you suppose I am going to bring my ropes, my windlass, and set it up, and go down there with my boy and let myself be bitten, perhaps, by your cursed dog for the pleasure of giving it back to you? You should not have thrown it down there."

She walked away, indignant. Four francs!

As soon as she entered the house she called Rose and told her of the quarryman's charges. Rose, always resigned, repeated:

"Four francs! That is a good deal of money, madame." Then she added: "If we could throw him something to eat, the poor dog, so he will not die of hunger."

Mme. Lefevre approved of this and was quite delighted. So they set out again with a big piece of bread and butter.

They cut it in mouthfuls, which they threw down one after the other, speaking by turns to Pierrot. As soon as the dog finished one piece he yelped for the next.

They returned that evening and the next day and every day. But they made only one trip.

One morning as they were just letting fall the first mouthful they suddenly heard a tremendous barking in the pit. There were two dogs there. Another had been thrown in, a large dog.

"Pierrot!" cried Rose. And Pierrot yelped and yelped. Then they began to throw down some food. But each time they noticed distinctly a terrible struggle going on, then plaintive cries from Pierrot, who had been bitten by his companion, who ate up everything as he was the stronger.

It was in vain that they specified, saying:

"That is for you, Pierrot." Pierrot evidently got nothing.

The two women, dumfounded, looked at each other and Mme. Lefevre said in a sour tone:

"I could not feed all the dogs they throw in there! We must give it up."

And, suffocating at the thought of all the dogs living at her expense, she went away, even carrying back what remained of the bread, which she ate as she walked along.

Rose followed her, wiping her eyes on the corner of her blue apron.

A NORMANDY JOKE

*J*t was a wedding procession that was coming along the road between the tall trees that bounded the farms and cast their shadow on the road. At the head were the bride and groom, then the family, then the invited guests, and last of all the poor of the neighborhood. The village urchins who hovered about the narrow road like flies ran in and out of the ranks or climbed up the trees to see it better.

The bridegroom was a good-looking young fellow, Jean Patu, the richest farmer in the neighborhood, but he was above all things, an ardent sportsman who seemed to take leave of his senses in order to satisfy that passion, and who spent large sums on his dogs, his keepers, his ferrets and his guns. The bride, Rosalie Roussel, had been courted by all the likely young fellows in the district, for they all thought her handsome and they knew that she would have a good dowry. But she had chosen Patu; partly, perhaps, because she liked him better than she did the others, but still more, like a careful Normandy girl, because he had more crown pieces.

As they entered the white gateway of the husband's farm, forty shots resounded without their seeing those who fired, as they were hidden in the ditches. The noise seemed to please the men, who were slouching along heavily in their best clothes, and Patu left his wife, and running up to a farm servant whom he perceived behind a tree, took his gun and fired a shot himself, as frisky as a young colt. Then they went on, beneath the apple trees which were heavy with fruit, through the high grass and through the midst of the calves, who looked at them with their great eyes, got up slowly and remained standing, with their muzzles turned toward the wedding party.

The men became serious when they came within measurable distance of the wedding dinner. Some of them, the rich ones, had on tall, shining silk hats, which seemed altogether out of place there; others had old head-coverings with a long nap, which might have been taken for moleskin, while the humblest among them wore caps. All the women had on shawls, which they wore loosely on their back, holding the tips ceremoniously under their arms. They were red, parti-colored, flaming shawls, and their brightness seemed to astonish the black fowls on the dung-heap, the ducks on the side of the pond and the pigeons on the thatched roofs.

The extensive farm buildings seemed to be waiting there at the end of that archway of apple trees, and a sort of vapor came out of open door and windows and an almost overpowering odor of eatables was exhaled from the vast building, from all its openings and from its very walls. The string of guests extended through the yard; but when the foremost of them reached the house, they broke the chain and dispersed, while those behind were still coming in at the open gate. The ditches were now lined with urchins and curious poor people, and the firing did not cease, but came from every side at once, and a cloud of smoke, and that odor which has the same intoxicating effect as absinthe, blended with the atmosphere. The women were shaking their dresses outside the door, to get rid of the dust, were undoing their cap-strings and pulling their shawls over their arms, and then they went into the house to lay them aside altogether for the time. The table was laid in the great kitchen that would hold a hundred persons; they sat down to dinner at two o'clock; and at eight o'clock they were still eating, and the men, in their shirt-sleeves, with their waist-coats unbuttoned and with red faces, were swallowing down the food and drink as if they had been whirlpools. The cider sparkled merrily, clear and golden in the large glasses, by the side of the dark, blood-colored wine, and between every dish they made a "hole," the Normandy hole, with a glass of brandy which inflamed the body and put foolish notions into the head. Low jokes were exchanged across the table until the whole arsenal of peasant wit was exhausted. For the last hundred years the same broad stories had served for similar occasions, and, although every one knew them, they still hit the mark and made both rows of guests roar with laughter.

At one end of the table four young fellows, who were neighbors, were preparing some practical jokes for the newly married couple, and they seemed to have got hold of a good one by the way they whispered and laughed, and suddenly one of them, profiting by a moment of silence, exclaimed: "The poachers will have a good time to-night, with this moon! I say, Jean, you will not be looking at the moon, will you?" The bridegroom turned to him quickly and replied: "Only let them come, that's all!" But the other young fellow began to laugh, and said: "I do not think you will pay much attention to them!"

The whole table was convulsed with laughter, so that the glasses shook, but the bridegroom became furious at the thought that anybody would profit by his wedding to come and poach on his land, and repeated: "I only say-just let them come!"

Then there was a flood of talk with a double meaning which made the bride blush somewhat, although she was trembling with expectation; and when they had emptied the kegs of brandy they all went to bed. The young couple went into their own room, which was on the ground floor, as most rooms in farmhouses are. As it was very warm, they opened the window and closed the shutters. A small lamp in bad taste, a present from the bride's father, was burning on the chest of drawers, and the bed stood ready to receive the young people.

The young woman had already taken off her wreath and her dress, and she was in her petticoat, unlacing her boots, while Jean was finishing his cigar and looking at her out of the corners of his eyes. Suddenly, with a brusque movement, like a man who is about to set to work, he took off his coat. She had already taken off her boots, and was now pulling off her stockings, and then she said to him: "Go and hide yourself behind the curtains while I get into bed."

He seemed as if he were about to refuse; but at last he did as she asked him, and in a moment she unfastened her petticoat, which slipped down, fell at her feet and lay on the ground. She left it there, stepped over it in her loose chemise and slipped into the bed, whose springs creaked beneath her weight. He immediately went up to the bed, and, stooping over his wife, he sought her lips, which she hid beneath the pillow, when a shot was heard in the distance, in the direction of the forest of Rapees, as he thought.

He raised himself anxiously, with his heart beating, and running to the window, he opened the shutters. The full moon flooded the yard with yellow light, and the reflection of the apple trees made black shadows at their feet, while in the distance the fields gleamed, covered with the ripe corn. But as he was leaning out, listening to every sound in the still night, two bare arms were put round his neck, and his wife whispered, trying to pull him back: "Do leave them alone; it has nothing to do with you. Come to bed."

He turned round, put his arms round her, and drew her toward him, but just as he was laying her on the bed, which yielded beneath her weight, they heard another report, considerably nearer this time, and Jean, giving way to his tumultuous rage, swore aloud: "Damn it! They will think I do not go out and see what it is because of you! Wait, wait a few minutes!" He put on his shoes again, took down his gun, which was always hanging within reach against the wall, and, as his wife threw herself on her knees in her terror, imploring him not to go, he hastily freed himself, ran to the window and jumped into the yard.

She waited one hour, two hours, until daybreak, but her husband did not return. Then she lost her head, aroused the house, related how angry Jean was, and said that he had gone after the poachers, and immediately all the male farm-servants, even the boys, went in search of their master. They found him two leagues from the farm, tied hand and foot, half dead with rage, his gun broken, his trousers turned inside out, and with three dead hares hanging round his neck, and a placard on his chest with these words: "Who goes on the chase loses his place."

In later years, when he used to tell this story of his wedding night, he usually added: "Ah! as far as a joke went it was a good joke. They caught me in a snare, as if I had been a rabbit, the dirty brutes, and they shoved my head into a bag. But if I can only catch them some day they had better look out for themselves!"

That is how they amuse themselves in Normandy on a wedding day.

FATHER MATTHEW

We had just left Rouen and were galloping along the road to Jumieges. The light carriage flew along across the level country. Presently the horse slackened his pace to walk up the hill of Cantelen.

One sees there one of the most magnificent views in the world. Behind us lay Rouen, the city of churches, with its Gothic belfries, sculptured like ivory trinkets; before us Saint Sever, the manufacturing suburb, whose thousands of smoking chimneys rise amid the expanse of sky, opposite the thousand sacred steeples of the old city.

On the one hand the spire of the cathedral, the highest of human monuments, on the other the engine of the power-house, its rival, and almost as high, and a metre higher than the tallest pyramid in Egypt.

Before us wound the Seine, with its scattered islands and bordered by white banks, covered with a forest on the right and on the left immense meadows, bounded by another forest yonder in the distance.

Here and there large ships lay at anchor along the banks of the wide river. Three enormous steam boats were starting out, one behind the other, for Havre, and a chain of boats, a bark, two schooners and a brig, were going upstream to Rouen, drawn by a little tug that emitted a cloud of black smoke.

My companion, a native of the country, did not glance at this wonderful landscape, but he smiled continually; he seemed to be amused at his thoughts. Suddenly he cried:

"Ah, you will soon see something comical—Father Matthew's chapel. That is a sweet morsel, my boy."

I looked at him in surprise. He continued:

"I will give you a whiff of Normandy that will stay by you. Father Matthew is the handsomest Norman in the province and his chapel is one of the wonders of the world, nothing more nor less. But I will first give you a few words of explanation.

"Father Matthew, who is also called Father 'La Boisson,' is an old sergeant-major who has come back to his native land. He combines in admirable proportions, making a perfect whole, the humbug of the old soldier and the sly roguery of the Norman. On his return to Normandy, thanks to influence and incredible cleverness, he was made doorkeeper of a votive chapel, a chapel dedicated to the Virgin and frequented chiefly by young women who have gone astray . . . . He composed and had painted a special prayer to his 'Good Virgin.' This prayer is a masterpiece of unintentional irony, of Norman wit, in which jest is blended with fear of the saint and with the superstitious fear of the secret influence of something. He has not much faith in his protectress, but he believes in her a little through prudence, and he is considerate of her through policy.

"This is how this wonderful prayer begins:

"'Our good Madame Virgin Mary, natural protectress of girl mothers in this land and all over the world, protect your servant who erred in a moment of forgetfulness . . .'

"It ends thus:

"'Do not forget me, especially when you are with your holy spouse, and intercede with God the Father that he may grant me a good husband, like your own.'

"This prayer, which was suppressed by the clergy of the district, is sold by him privately, and is said to be very efficacious for those who recite it with unction.

"In fact he talks of the good Virgin as the valet de chambre of a redoubted prince might talk of his master who confided in him all his little private secrets. He knows a number of amusing anecdotes at his expense which he tells confidentially among friends as they sit over their glasses.

"But you will see for yourself.

"As the fees coming from the Virgin did not appear sufficient to him, he added to the main figure a little business in saints. He has them all, or nearly all. There was not room enough in the chapel, so he stored them in the wood-shed and brings them forth as soon as the faithful ask for them. He carved these little wooden statues himself—they are comical in the extreme—and painted them all bright green one year when they were painting his house. You know that saints cure diseases, but each saint has his specialty, and you must not confound them or make any blunders. They are as jealous of each other as mountebanks.

"In order that they may make no mistake, the old women come and consult Matthew.

"'For diseases of the ear which saint is the best?'

"'Why, Saint Osyme is good and Saint Pamphilius is not bad.'

But that is not all.

"As Matthew has some time to spare, he drinks; but he drinks like a professional, with conviction, so much so that he is intoxicated regularly every evening. He is drunk, but he is aware of it. He is so well aware of it that he notices each day his exact degree of intoxication. That is his chief occupation; the chapel is a secondary matter.

"And he has invented—listen and catch on—he has invented the 'Saoulometre.'

"There is no such instrument, but Matthew's observations are as precise as those of a mathematician. You may hear him repeating incessantly: 'Since Monday I have had more than forty-five,' or else 'I was between fifty-two and fifty-eight,' or else 'I had at least sixty-six to seventy,' or 'Hullo, cheat, I thought I was in the fifties and here I find I had had seventy-five!'

"He never makes a mistake.

"He declares that he never reached his limit, but as he acknowledges that his observations cease to be exact when he has passed ninety, one cannot depend absolutely on the truth of that statement.

"When Matthew acknowledges that he has passed ninety, you may rest assured that he is blind drunk.

"On these occasions his wife, Melie, another marvel, flies into a fury. She waits for him at the door of the house, and as he enters she roars at him:

"'So there you are, slut, hog, giggling sot!'

"Then Matthew, who is not laughing any longer, plants himself opposite her and says in a severe tone:

"'Be still, Melie; this is no time to talk; wait till to-morrow.'

"If she keeps on shouting at him, he goes up to her and says in a shaky voice:

"'Don't bawl any more. I have had about ninety; I am not counting any more. Look out, I am going to hit you!'

"Then Melie beats a retreat.

"If, on the following day, she reverts to the subject, he laughs in her face and says:

"'Come, come! We have said enough. It is past. As long as I have not reached my limit there is no harm done. But if I go past that, I will allow you to correct me, my word on it!'"

We had reached the top of the hill. The road entered the delightful forest of Roumare.

Autumn, marvellous autumn, blended its gold and purple with the remaining traces of verdure. We passed through Duclair.

Then, instead of going on to Jumieges, my friend turned to the left and, taking a crosscut, drove in among the trees.

And presently from the top of a high hill we saw again the magnificent valley of the Seine and the winding river beneath us.

At our right a very small slate-covered building, with a bell tower as large as a sunshade, adjoined a pretty house with green Venetian blinds, and all covered with honeysuckle and roses.

"Here are some friends!" cried a big voice, and Matthew appeared on the threshold. He was a man about sixty, thin and with a goatee and long, white mustache.

My friend shook him by the hand and introduced me, and Matthew took us into a clean kitchen, which served also as a dining-room. He said:

"I have no elegant apartment, monsieur. I do not like to get too far away from the food. The saucepans, you see, keep me company." Then, turning to my friend:

"Why did you come on Thursday? You know quite well that this is the day I consult my Guardian Saint. I cannot go out this afternoon."

And running to the door, he uttered a terrific roar: "Melie!" which must have startled the sailors in the ships along the stream in the valley below.

Melie did not reply.

Then Matthew winked his eye knowingly.

"She is not pleased with me, you see, because yesterday I was in the nineties."

My friend began to laugh. "In the nineties, Matthew! How did you manage it?"

"I will tell you," said Matthew. "Last year I found only twenty rasieres (an old dry measure) of apricots. There are no more, but those are the only things to make cider of. So I made some, and yesterday I tapped the barrel. Talk of nectar! That was nectar. You shall tell me what you think of it. Polyte was here, and we sat down and drank a glass and another without being satisfied (one could go on drinking it until to-morrow), and at last, with glass after glass, I felt a chill at my stomach. I said to Polyte: 'Supposing we drink a glass of cognac to warm ourselves?' He agreed. But this cognac, it sets you on fire, so that we had to go back to the cider. But by going from chills to heat and heat to chills, I saw that I was in the nineties. Polyte was not far from his limit."

The door opened and Melie appeared. At once, before bidding us good-day, she cried:

"Great hog, you have both of you reached your limit!"

"Don't say that, Melie; don't say that," said Matthew, getting angry. "I have never reached my limit."

They gave us a delicious luncheon outside beneath two lime trees, beside the little chapel and overlooking the vast landscape. And Matthew told us, with a mixture of humor and unexpected credulity, incredible stories of miracles.

We had drunk a good deal of delicious cider, sparkling and sweet, fresh and intoxicating, which he preferred to all other drinks, and were smoking our pipes astride our chairs when two women appeared.

They were old, dried up and bent. After greeting us they asked for Saint Blanc. Matthew winked at us as he replied:

"I will get him for you." And he disappeared in his wood shed. He remained there fully five minutes. Then he came back with an expression of consternation. He raised his hands.

"I don't know where he is. I cannot find him. I am quite sure that I had him." Then making a speaking trumpet of his hands, he roared once more:

"Meli-e-a!"

"What's the matter?" replied his wife from the end of the garden.

"Where's Saint Blanc? I cannot find him in the wood shed."

Then Melie explained it this way:

"Was not that the one you took last week to stop up a hole in the rabbit hutch?"

Matthew gave a start.

"By thunder, that may be!" Then turning to the women, he said: "Follow me."

They followed him. We did the same, almost choking with suppressed laughter.

Saint Blanc was indeed stuck into the earth like an ordinary stake, covered with mud and dirt, and forming a corner for the rabbit hutch.

As soon as they perceived him, the two women fell on their knees, crossed themselves and began to murmur an "Oremus." But Matthew darted toward them.

"Wait," he said, "you are in the mud; I will get you a bundle of straw."

He went to fetch the straw and made them a priedieu. Then, looking at his muddy saint and doubtless afraid of bringing discredit on his business, he added:

"I will clean him off a little for you."

He took a pail of water and a brush and began to scrub the wooden image vigorously, while the two old women kept on praying.

When he had finished he said:

"Now he is all right." And he took us back to the house to drink another glass.

As he was carrying the glass to his lips he stopped and said in a rather confused manner:

"All the same, when I put Saint Blanc out with the rabbits I thought he would not make any more money. For two years no one had asked for him. But the saints, you see, they are never out of date."